QuixotiQ

QuixotiQ

Ali Al Saeed

iUniverse, Inc.
New York Lincoln Shanghai

QuixotiQ

All Rights Reserved © 2004 by Ali Abdulrazaq Al Saeed

No part of this book may be reproduced or transmitted in any form or by any means, graphic, electronic, or mechanical, including photocopying, recording, taping, or by any information storage retrieval system, without the written permission of the publisher.

iUniverse, Inc.

For information address:
iUniverse, Inc.
2021 Pine Lake Road, Suite 100
Lincoln, NE 68512
www.iuniverse.com

ISBN: 0-595-32761-3

Printed in the United States of America

To dreams…

Acknowledgments

Firstly I would like to thank Allah for giving me my heart's desires. I owe my parents—Mama and Baba—a great deal for their support and encouragement. My big sister Hana and my brother-in-law, Ali Salman, I will be forever indebt to them. They have all gone further than I had imagined they would to help me achieve my goal and make my dream come true.

I would also like to thank all the people who have contributed one way or the other in making this book as best as it could ever become and supported my ideas and ambitions. But most of all, I owe this book and my life to someone who was always very special to me and who has a warm place in my heart, to the woman I love and cherish, Karen Warner, who's given me more than I hoped for and have stood by me through thick and thin and made me what I am today.

You have been my inspiration, my motivation, my rock, my courage, my love. And, let's face it, if it weren't for your brilliant editing skills, this book wouldn't have been half as good as it is!

Thank you.

Chapter 1

▼

It is four in the morning following one humid and silent August night and Guy Kelton has not fallen asleep yet. For several hours he has been twisting and turning in bed trying to find the best sleeping position, keeping his eyes shut with relentless effort.

Every now and then he would open them wide and for few seconds stare at the darkness surrounding him, seeing murky blue objects so hard to identify surrounding him. For a fraction of a second he would recognize these objects as other than they truly are. This fraction though, seems to last long enough to startle away any drowsiness he would have been feeling. Things would appear monstrous to him in this lone fraction of a second, demonic and harmful. Sometimes he sees what would look like a horrid face staring with rigid large eyes at him, or some malign alien creature ready to attack him, gore him and devour him, and sometimes he thinks that the cupboard or closet are coming alive, somehow, to come and get him.

Every night he watches late night television—Conon O'Brien is his favorite, never failing to make him laugh—or he reads whatever magazine he can get his hands on until one or two in the morning before attempting to go to sleep. Sometimes when he is on his bed, praying for some sleep, he takes off the blanket, other times he wraps himself in it. Sometimes sleeps on his belly, other times on his back but he rarely sleeps on his sides, a habit that he has not understood and one that keeps him wondering whether other people were like him when it comes to sleep.

It's strange how a man can yearn so much for something, want it so badly to a degree where the soul of this man no longer accepts it, even if and when it arrives.

When a person concentrates so much on getting something, he or she would most probably not get it…in the end. Sometimes one tries so hard to get it that one gets sidetracked…and loses one's self to some unknown fate which one have not taken heed of before, not considered or even could imagine. This has been the case for Guy for so long. All the things he yearns for he does not get. Sleep, money, a better job, a woman to love, satisfaction. Life. Just life.

Now he lays on his belly, again. Both hands slipped under the pillow. Eyes shut and mind thinking, perhaps pretending to be dreaming. For these long endless hours waiting for sleep he makes up a parallel story for his life. He imagines how nice it would be if he had a woman to fall deeply in love with and imagine what great sex he would be having with her. He imagines how wonderful it would feel if he quit his current job and moved from this stupid, clumsy town to another and get some other job. Some nights, like this night, he masturbates out of loneliness, and feels sorry for himself.

One night, not very long ago, he imagined the perfect life…

He had the girl of his dreams, a girl as romantic as he, a girl so beautiful and soft and kind. A girl who understood him and knew his wants and needs, a girl who is blond, tall, sexy and faithful, and above all, a girl who deserved his love.

In this imaginative life he was able to do whatever he pleased, work in the profession that comforts him—perhaps even become the professional ball player he's always dreamed he'd be as a kid—living in a city full of beautiful and nice people, a city with tall buildings and colorful markets and green streets. A city where the sun shines so bright and clouds as fluffy as cotton and as white as snow hover around, blocking the rays of the sun as they pass by for short moments, and where the sky is as blue as it could ever get.

But then again, this remains fiction and imagination. Nothing more, nothing less. Guy would live this imaginative life through until he fell asleep, memorizing every little detail, going as far as thinking of the little silver pen which his girlfriend gave him on his 25th birthday, placed in the black plastic pen holder, on the office desk made of oak wood, in the small office room, at his big well furnished two-room apartment, in a tall pretty building on the street full of green trees and colorful flowers, opposite the river which is separating the two sides of the city…of dreams.

Just life. All he ever wanted.

Now, it was getting nearer to five and Guy is finally asleep. He sleeps and sleeps, silently in the fading blackness. Then he dreams. Every single night he dreams and every single dream is more twisted and horrid and frustrating than the one before. He is haunted by dreams. His mind never fails once to produce a remarkable one, but then again all things dream are remarkable for Guy. This particular night he had a most awkward dream.

It was the times of the Gothic. There was a small kingdom that had a king, who was corrupt and evil. The King lived in a huge castle on a top of a rocky mountain. And there was a tower built in that castle, under the orders of the King, so tall and high it touched the sky and went through the clouds. It was built so that no human can ever reach it.

Strangely, the King lived all alone. He was of late age. Ageing faster than he had liked. He did not have any guards, as he was always afraid that one day someone close to him might betray him. The Kingdom was very green, deep forest filled the landscape. The land's people were helpless and indifferent to their own fates, all busy trying to make a living and earn a little food to consume and that was all they thought of, they never cared for what the King did nor wanted to care.

Guy was there, with his elder brother Morris and another person who he could not see—he was there without a tangible figure—but was someone he felt very close to, both of whom he has not seen in many years. They came to the land seeking the King. The three of them came to bring down the king and end the corruption, end his era of neglecting the people and abuse of power and sinister control and to awaken them.

No one gave them heed. No one followed them. Still no one cared.

Then the three of them with the help of a giant raven, which was brought by the Gods of the time, were able to act as they wanted. The raven flew them up the skies to the top of the tower, where the King was in hiding after hearing about these three who were coming to assassinate him. They got into the tower through its small window and captured the King without much difficulty. There were no guards to fight or beasts to slay and the King did not seem willing to put up a fight of his own.

Morris took a rope and prepared a noose for the King to be hanged.

"This is what you deserve," said the unseen figure to the King, who was helpless and seemed to have accepted his fate.

The black raven was hovering around the tower as the three men noticed a roaring sound coming from outside. The noise grew slowly bigger and louder. Guy looked out through the window to see the people of the land gathering and shouting in favor of the heroic men.

"*Kill him, slay him, hang him, behead him.*" shouted the people.

Morris resumed his mission and placed the noose on the neck of the King and forwarded him to the window. The King looked down and he was scared, terrified. He was very scared of his own people, he was scared of the height and he was scared of dying. Not much was said by anyone. Until the King spoke these words "You will kill your own father then, eh?"

Saying this the King glanced at the faces of the three men. They all wore expressions of shock and surprise and amazement.

"You are our father!" exclaimed Guy, bewildered.

"That cannot be!" interrupted Morris, "Because I am not his son, nor are you my brother," looking at Guy, whose face whitened and shrunk.

For some unknown reason they all were convinced so easily and believed the King.

"It should make no difference. You are a sinner. You should die," said Guy finally. Guy, just before pushing the King to meet his death, suddenly found the King turning into a small wooden doll. It didn't make much sense to anyone but they resumed with the proceeding and dropped the King doll from the window and everyone was happy, jeering and cheering as they saw him falling down and meeting his demise, breaking and shattering into pieces.

Before he knows it Guy is awake. His eyes have just opened and he is back in the real world. He doesn't know what happened, he doesn't know if the King was truly his father in the dream. He doesn't know how on earth the King turned into a wooden doll, or why he was there with Morris in first place or whom the faceless figure was that he felt such strong connection to but didn't recognize. He wants these questions to be answered, but who would know? But then he thinks this was just a dream that means nothing. All dreams mean nothing. He never wants to believe that dreams mean something, but he is never certain no matter how much he tries to convince himself.

He hates waking up in the middle of a dream. Maybe there's not enough sleep time that he has in the night or any other night. Just three to four hours of sleep in a day is probably not enough to lead a happy life. It is already quarter to nine when he rose from bed, leaving him only fifteen minutes to go to work. His head thick and heavy as a stone. The post-dream-post-sleep feeling is sickening to him. The whole thing makes him feel terrible. The hours of waiting for sleep to come, the unfinished weird dreams, the few hours of sleep. It all adds up to making him the worst man in the universe in the morning. You just wouldn't want to be in his face then.

He collects his strength and pulls his body up from the bed with as much difficulty as moving a brick wall with your bare hands. He feels a rush of thoughts flowing through his brains so fast for a second he feels he might faint, but fortunately he doesn't.

Images of the dream flash up but he doesn't think much of it, he only tries to concentrate on getting up and out of bed. After picking himself up, everything else is done in sheer automated mechanism, these compulsory chores are to him tool of torture. He performs them involuntarily and with disgruntled attitude. Every morning in the same order. His mind follows that order sacredly.

1. Peeing.

2. Washing face.

3. Brushing teeth.

4. Combing hair.

5. Putting on clothes.

6. Sometimes have breakfast.

He doesn't care much about having breakfast. Fact is he can't remember when the last had a decent breakfast, since he has left his home. Most mornings he would imagine the table full of all he desires, just like that which his mother used to prepare each morning for him and his father and his brother.

There would be milk, juice, cereals, jams, toast, eggs, butter, cheese…every important element forming the perfect breakfast meal. When he was young his father did well and he tried his best to cover all their needs but then, as he grew older, things started to worsen for some reason little Guy could not understand. He knew something was wrong, because breakfasts weren't the same anymore. Slowly they became only milk and cheese and buttered toasts and scarcely would there be eggs. That's when he knew he had no intentions to stay there.

His studio apartment is a mess. Few furniture items thrown around, actually the place had its own bed, sofa, table and chair. A 25' television set, a video and a stereo, which he bought from the flea market, are all kept in one corner. He'd bought one item each month until he completed his life-essentials collection. He'd started with the television, then the stereo and the video-player after much hesitation.

He doesn't think about his place much. He doesn't care.

Guy goes out to the street to walk to his workplace, just five minutes away, if he takes huge and quick steps. He run-walks, that's what he calls it. On his way to work he uses the same routes, passing the same places and seeing the same faces.

After a while of doing that he grew a habit of not paying heed to anything or anyone around him. He would just look down to the ground and run-walk until he reached his destination. He found it to be a very efficient way to lose the sense of time; it would make the distances seem shorter. He even used to do that while he was still going to school. He and his big brother went to the same school and walked together to and from it almost every day. But they never talked much while walking along side each other. They just ran-walked.

It was only on rainy days that their father or their mother, before her health crippled her movements, came to pick them up from school. Rarely, finding one of their parents parked near the school gate waiting for them would surprise them. When that happened both would feel relieved that they would not have to go through that automatic procedure of walking the same size steps along the exact same paths.

Guy would sometimes concentrate so hard at walking over the exact path he and his brother has taken the day before. He would look for little things on the ground, things like decaying gum or a little branch or a dead leaf. One day he'd even noticed his own footprints over the sandy tight passage leading from the main road to his neighborhood, left behind from a previous excursion.

Now, it's seven minutes past nine. And life even at this peak hour of the morning is picking up lazily.

The town he is living in is mostly quiet; people seem more dead than alive. Nothing exciting happens here. Everything is small, the buildings are short and the streets are narrow and unclean and Guy has only been out of it once, only once in all his twenty-four years on earth.

While he was walking he realises something he thinks is unique. He realises that it is impossible for anyone to recall the exact words said in a dream; not only the words but the writings as well.

In a dream one does not actually read anything, but one's mind convinces oneself that one is reading in the dream. Even if one did read while dreaming, the chances of remembering the sentences are next to nil, virtually non-existent. You would see the characters and words in the back of your head after waking up, but these would never make any sense: just a collection of words forming meaningless sentences. He wonders why is that so? It is really mind-boggling and he reflects over it much. Why is the brain able to recollect only the images of a dream, and only fractions of these images for that matter?

All of a sudden his mind leads him to think further of the dream about the king. Could it be that it was the leftover memories of a past life that my soul has lived? Come to think of it, it could be the only explanation, to have strange places and strange faces never seen before in your life, but which are familiar while dreaming.

Faces of strangers in our dreams! Where do they come from? Memories. It could be the face of the old man selling newspapers at the corner, the little boy always playing at the street on his bike, the man who wanted to sell you the lottery tickets you never wanted, the cute waitress who brought you back your change after a nice hot cup of coffee, or the faces of the many people who simply pass by you walking.

That's the main reason Guy stares down while walking, he does not want any more strange faces to invade his sub-consciousness and hide to surface in another freakish dream.

Guy knows he was supposed to be close to his destination now, but when he looks up, he was surprised at what he saw. He finds himself in an alley with two endless walls stretching up until his eyes cannot see them anymore. He is there alone, everyone is gone, and everything familiar to him has vanished. He is in some place he has never been before, someplace strange to his eyes. He looks around. There is not a soul that he could ask about where he is. But after a short period of time Guy notices a dark figure approaching him slowly, making an echoing sound with each step it takes. It seems to be a man.

"Sir, where is this place? I believe I have lost my way?" he askes the man who is coming closer.

The man without replying stopped, just about ten paces away. Behind him Guy sees a huge gate made of black metal, a cold shiver runs through his body at the sight of it.

There is something fearful and dark about that gate. Although the thought of turning around and returning the same path crosses Guy's mind several times, he doesn't. He just stands there, amazed and yet again puzzled, as if he were in a dream, helpless.

"Go back boy. You are not supposed to be here," says the man. His voice is hollow and he looks very old but strong. He is tall and has long grey hair and is of medium build.

"Who are you? What is this place?"

"You have no right to be here young man. Leave now for I run of patience quickly." says the man in a strict manner.

"No." says Guy, surprising himself in doing so. "I want to know. Don't threaten me, old man! I think I'm lost. Where does that gate lead? Let me through," A strong sense of invincibility washes over him.

"Very well, boy. But you won't like it much. I have warned you." The man turns back and heads towards the gate.

"Follow me,"

Guy follows him, he feels his heart bouncing menacingly and sweat starting to run down his forehead. It is exciting and frightening at the same time. It is the fear of the unknown and the excitement of the unexpected.

They reach the gate.

"If you really want to know, then I am afraid you will have to go in on your own, Guy Jay Kelton," the old man.

Guy is not surprised by the fact the old man knew his name, but it is the way the old man said the last two names that irks him. He now expects anything to happen, filled with the sort of limitless possibilities one finds in dreams. He concentrates on the gate. It is huge and dark. It seemes, for a crazy second, that it calls him by name, enticing him to come forward, to go through, it but it isn't calling. It can't be.

Finally, Guy, after much hesitation, stretches his right hand and puts it against the gate to try and push it. At this moment even he himself does not know what he is thinking, it is as if his mind was temporarily jammed, blocked, no access.

He glances at the sky, it is still grey, but now there are a few little blue clouds. He stares at the old man and then at the gate. He then closes his eyes and walks ahead.

Momentarily, everything went black. Guy notices a sound, getting louder and louder...He opens his eyes to find himself in the middle of the road. A car is only inches away from him; its driver very upset at something. He is honking a lot.

He looks around himself in disbelief. The gate was gone and the old man has disappeared. A moment of relief. "What just happened to me?" He asks himself, still standing, bemused, in the middle of the road, as if all his senses are dumb and numb. He looks to the left and there a man is shouting—might have been swearing—apparently at him. Guy ignores him. He looks up to the sky one more time to make sure it is all back to normal. It is. More relief!

Guy turns around and starts walking, with heavy steps and shoulders, back towards his home again.

Chapter 2

As she looks into the mirror, she wondered and she pondered, "What reflection does this mirror possess? Why does it have our reflection? Which of us does the mirror portray?"

It was a mystery, she reckoned, how bizarre we feel when we look at ourselves and perceive ourselves differently every time: sometimes it feels as if looking at a complete stranger, or sometimes a long lost friend or perhaps even your worst enemy. But she always admired her mirror self. She admired her own eyes, her hair, her white skin, her nose, her lips and her body.

Oh, how wonderful I am.

She took a few steps to the left and looked out the window. Everything seemed slow and lifeless, even though there were people walking and cars passing.

She looked down to the far right corner across the street and there he was again, the old man in the flower shop, who spends his whole days watering them and taking care of them, moving so slow, that you would think a turtle would move quicker than him. He is always alone. She would buy a rose from him almost everyday, every time a different color. It would make him so happy. It also made her happy.

As she was posing, a little bird flew near and landed on the edge of the window she was standing behind. She looked at the bird and praised its beauty, its freedom and lightness in movement. She loved the way birds moved and walked. But they didn't walk, did they? They hopped. That bird now hopped from end to end, its head cocking in every direction. It seemed to be in search of something.

"Oh, birdie. If you only knew." she said as she put her palm against the cool window glass to touch the bird, "If you only knew how innocent and pretty you are."

The bird looked at her, one small quick glance, and then flew off. The sound of the door opening nosily startled her. Christina smiled and wished that she could do what birds can do, fly far away as soon as they feel a danger or a hazard is nearing, because that's how she's been feeling lately.

"Hey Chrissy! What's up?" said a young lady in blue and grey, as she entered the toilet opening the door noisily.

"Hi Mandy." replied Christina with a sigh, and added as she turned back to the window "I was just observing our lively and wonderfully active world out through the window!" she said sarcastically.

"Well, early this morning there was this crazy bloke walking down the street. He had a strange walk and he was trying to cross the street while the light was red. He was walking like a zombie or something, y'know, with his hands reaching out, head looking up and eyes shut and all!" she stopped to catch her breath, then added "You should've seen him," bursting into a restrained giggle, getting closer to the mirror to look at herself. She brushed her hair with her hand.

"Oh and by the by, the boss was looking for you. You ought to get back to your desk."

"Oh no, sweet lord! What does the Bitch want from me now?" whispered Christina. She left the toilet with great uneasiness.

She was of medium height and build, with hair as brown as coffee beans, reaching her shoulders. Her face was long and her eyes were big and hazel. She had some Eastern looks in her. When she walked she could sense eyes, men's and women's, following her every step. She is twenty-five years of age. And she was shy and dreamy.

"Hey...Wood!" Came a yelp, as she arrived at her cubicle.

"Yes?" she replied, adjusting her silver shiny seat so she could sit comfortably at her little desk. She is a secretary. She has worked as a secretary for so long, she feels it's the only thing she has done since the day she was born.

She looked to her right, where she had put a pink rose in a white mug; she bought it that morning from the old man down the street. She loves pink roses. They are beautiful, smell great and calm her whenever she is nervous or distressed. She would take a sniff and swim into the land of colorful roses and get intoxicated by the smell.

She was not paying attention to the woman in the nice business suit, whose big gob was open wide barking out meaningless words. To her this woman does not even exist, she is nothing but a colorful shadow. Christina was in a dreamy mood. Now nothing surrounding her was there anymore. Everything else seemed unfocused and unimportant, everything but the pink rose in the white mug.

"I wish I was a rose," she said in a low voice, and all the meaningless words stopped for a little while.

"Yes. I will probably get cut and taken away from my fellow roses but I will at least please someone, someone unhappy and miserable, make them feel comfortable when they smell me, make their eyes see nothing but beauty when they look at me, inside of me. I will die sooner, but I will die happy and I would hurt those who wish to destroy me with my sharp little thorns!"

As she was saying this, calmly, she held the rose and then she sniffed it and smiled. Life seemed to have stopped, the whole world stopped for a minute as she suddenly found her self in an endless field of pink roses. A garden so vast and big it stretched till she couldn't see it anymore.

She was in the middle of that garden, wearing a cute little pink dress. The world around her smelled wonderful and the sky was white and the clouds were pink. The smell made her feel so pleased and wonderful and young. In the field there was no one but herself, for a moment only. She looked around and then looked ahead and saw another woman; she wore a black dress and was upset about something, and as she rambled on and on, little by little, the white sky turned a bit grey, the clouds became grey florescent lights and the ground turned from a roses field to a miserable blue office carpet and the woman she saw was actually her bitchy boss.

Christina hated having a boss, hated the idea of having someone telling you what to do and making orders. All bosses are bitches, Christina thinks, they are all the same; eager to exploit their authority. She never hated them personally though. Actually, sometimes she would feel sorry for them, for having to be such despicable people because of their jobs.

"Here, smell the rose. You'll feel better." Christina said.

"You are so pathetic Wood." Said the boss, storming out of the office.

Christina held the rose close to her chest; "So are you." she whispered and then started revolving her chair, just like a child. Christina had this little child within her, she doesn't care about things much but she gets upset easily too. She made the first circle, the second and in the third she saw another woman figure which looked like Mandy in front of her, and she stopped.

"Oh, I thought it was you!" she exclaimed.

"Yes. It's me. Now tell me. What are you going to do?"

"Well, I have some papers I should type up I guess and…"

"Chrissy? It's not funny. This is serious. How will you manage yourself?"

"Eh? I don't think I understand you."

"The Bitch just fired you Chrissy. You are fired."

"What? I..."

"Oh, God. Don't tell me, you were in Rose Land!?"

Christina was shocked, or at least she thought she ought to be. "I wasn't paying attention. Should I panic?" she asked her friend.

"Uh, how would I know Chrissy? I am not you."

"Well, I guess I shouldn't. It wouldn't make much of a difference now, would it?" she stood up, with her rose in her hand, and walked out of the office. She just wanted to get away. Now that she lost her job, and that after her boyfriend cheated on her and dumped her before she even knew a few days ago.

"Are you going to be all right?" asked Mandy, knowing that the reply would not mean anything at that moment. But there was no reply anyway.

"Oh, you are so naive Christina Haywood. So sweetly naïve," she said shaking her head.

Christina went out to the street, walking briskly. She was angry; she was upset, she was even panicking—something she hates going through—as the realization of what had happened sunk in.

It was hot; the sun threw its bright golden rays on everything, the sky was pale and clear, no clouds. She put on her sunshades and walked and walked, picking the leaves of the pink rose one by one, until she found her self in front of the old man's flower store. She looked at the store, the shelves filled with different sorts and types of flowers and roses.

"Hello dear love." said the old man. His voice sounds like when someone talks while he has water in his mouth.

"Would you like another rose?"

"No. No, thank you. I'm fine." she said and then added after a little pause "No, actually, I'm not."

"Oh, what harm has come upon you my dear? Please speak. Do not feel uneasy. I am like an uncle to you," he said in his foreign accent. He was honest and comforting and always seemed interested in young people. I guess all old people are like that: Sweet, kind and gentle and fragile.

"Well, I was wondering. Don't you have anyone in your life? A wife, a friend, a son, anyone?"

"Uh, the ultimate question of the young to the lonely old. No I don't, not because I don't have any, just because I don't want to have anything to do with them. I know you will ask, why? Because people only bring pain to each other and because I know that no one wants to have an old man around these days. I know that if I stayed with my son and his wife, they will hate me and detest me even more. I will be an added weight on their shoulder. I know that if I had a wife, I won't be able to please or satisfy her and I know if I had a friend they will always want more from me than I could ever give." he said, as he picked up a few daisies and handed them over to Christina.

"Forgive me. I am senselessly rambling. What's your name young child?"

"Christina."

"What a wonderful name. Listen Christina, what ever it is that bothers you, forget it and go on with your life. Never ever look back. All the things that are meant to be, will be. Don't worry, everything will be just fine. Eventually."

She looked down at the daisies, sniffed them and held them close to her breast. She turned away and resumed her walk.

"I wish it could be that easy, I really wish it could."

Chapter 3

▼

The ocean was big and blue. Parts of it had a greenish shade near the coastline. He was high, so high up in the sky, looking down at the few houses, at the streets and bridges of this unfamiliar place. A beautiful island. He was hearing voices, a conversation, between his mother and little sister, but they weren't there! He couldn't see them, and he couldn't understand what they were saying.

For a second he thought he was in a helicopter, but he wasn't. He was just floating in the sky. He can feel the breezy air brushing over his bare chest. At first he wasn't scared, everything was calm and tranquil, peaceful and wonderful. But then the waters grew angry, creating giant, menacing waves, lunging on the little houses down below. There were sands from the beach also moving and attacking and destroying, like walls made of sandstorms. It was all strange and weird, the pace in which things turned around disturbed him and took him by surprise. There were fluffy stripes of sand marking the waters, just like clouds marking the sky. It felt terrible to see homes brought down and drowned, eaten by the giant waves.

But now it felt like watching a movie, furthermore, it felt like it's not real and after another few seconds it felt like a dream…and opening his eyes slowly, yes it was a dream.

Patrick Roymint, tucked underneath his white sheets, with one of his legs out in the open, his right hand bent and below his chest and his other hand flipped to his back, started to wake.

It was three in the afternoon and he hadn't done anything but lie in bed and sleep all day, just like yesterday, and the day before. He quit his job at the diner because he just got bored of it, after working there for seven months. Now he does nothing. And nothing is there in the small room he is living in, except an old bed, an old small TV, an old fridge, an old radio and an old couch.

His mother and sister died drowning after their little boat flipped over during a sea outing on a stormy September day. It was a dark day for the Roymint family and certainly not a day Patrick likes to remember. But it haunts him every day and every night.

The weather that day was fine in the early hours of the morning but then the winds and waves went mad. His father, who was a helicopter rescuer, failed to save them on that ominous day. He could not find them in the waters; their bodies were never retrieved. It devastated him, crushed his will to live and sucked the spirit dry out of him. On the first anniversary of that tragedy, Patrick's father killed himself; he couldn't cope with failing them. Patrick was left all alone.

It's been twenty years since all that happened. He was seven years old. And until this day Patrick does not understand how he was able to go through all of this alone.

He lived with his uncle, Matt, and his family of four, in the dwindling suburbs of Blossomville for the first ten years after his father killed himself. He left his uncle's house soon after his eighteenth birthday and after completing his high school education, moved into the city to begin a new life, away from what reminded him of his long-lost family. Three months after moving, he met Mandy.

The phone rings. Patrick hesitates to pick it up. His head aching and his sight still not clear, he adjusts himself and leans toward the red phone on the desk beside his bed. "Hello", he says.

"Hey Pat! Wake up," said a feminine voice.

Patrick ran his hand through his hair and then downwards onto his mouth to keep it from yawning. He doesn't reply and waits for the next line.

"It's me!"

"I know."

"Come on, pick your fat bum up and do something for life's sake!"

"Mandy, look; just leave me alone OK?" he said with a grunt.

"You know I won't!" she said playfully "Listen, we should meet tonight. I heard they are looking for a driver for our delivery department; you might as well try to get it. Oh, and my best friend just got fired, so I am feeling a bit terrible."

Patrick did not hear the next part, or maybe he didn't care to. "I told you I don't want to work Mandy…and no, we should not meet tonight. Just forget about me for a while, leave me in peace." he said, as he drew back the phone to place it back.

He looked at the little yellow alarm clock; it indicated ten minutes past three in the afternoon. For a little while he sat up straight on the quirky bed, looking at the ground and his feet, and he remembered and he wets. Silently. Then loudly, he wept harder, alone in this forlorn place.

It was on this day, at this exact time that that accident happened and he lost his whole family. The image of his long gone mother and his beautiful little sister Karla—she was only twelve—resurfaces once again. He sees their faces, and his father's.

His father, Robert George Patrick, was always a fair father, a man who believed in God and who believed in himself and his family. Patrick remembers how his father hated to fail in his missions, when he lost someone in a rescue operation he would feel miserable and not eat for days. But that did not happen often, his father rarely failed. He also did not think for a single moment that he would lose his family like that.

"You know son, each man would have to face one disastrous period in his lifetime, like a phantom monster. You either kill it or let it gnaw on you alive until there's nothing left of you but a hollow skeleton," said his father once.

Well, his father seemed to have let that monster eat him. Somehow he gave into it, and Patrick would forever wonder why.

Patrick went out to the narrow balcony of his apartment, leans on the metal fence, looking down the street. There were a few people passing by, all seemed lost, all seemed unfocused, all seemed, to him, unaware of their destinations.

He gazed further ahead and then up to the sky. The sun was still warm and yellow. He gets in again, walks to the table and picks his pack of cigarettes and trots to the balcony again. Patrick pulls out a cigarette, slips it in between his dry lips, no lighter. He growls. Once again he goes inside and looks for his little gas lighter. Where is the little motherfucker? He shouted.

Patrick's parents did not smoke. None of them did. He did not have friends who smoked. But he did. He started after the accident, even though he was so young. His father always told him to leave it because it will ruin his life.

"You'll end up coughing your lungs out, you idiot!" he yelled at him.

Patrick thought it was normal for his father to be upset because all parents tend to care for their children. Well, most of them. But with his father, during that time, it was half-hearted parenting. He was losing his own battles. He couldn't fight his son's as well.

As he took a peak under his bed, looking for the lighter, there was a knock at the door. He stops the search operation, sitting on his knees, hands on his waist. Looking puzzled—Who the hell would that be?

"Open up, it's me." said the person behind the door.

Uh, of course. Mandy. Who else? He stands up and walks towards the door. Another heavy knock. He draws the cigarette out of his mouth.

"Okay, I heard you." as he opened it fiercely he was greeted with a lovely smile, all innocent and pure.

"Hello stranger," she said, "I finished early so I thought I could drop by."

"Do you have a light?"

"Patty! You know I don't smoke, and neither should you."

"Damn it! Can't anything go right in my flipping life? I just want to smoke this fucking cigarette." he was agitated. A headache was creeping in. He was in a foul mood. .

"You don't have to swear Pat. Just calm down. I brought some vanilla and chocolate ice-cream for you." she said with a cool tone.

She was always like that, cool and calm and easy, especially with him. She loved him, so much, no matter what.

She sat on the table, pulled out the ice-cream box and scooped some out with a plastic spoon she bought with her. Patrick doesn't have a lot of spoons, or knives, or forks, or dishes. He doesn't eat a lot. He couldn't bother. That's why he is becoming thinner every passing day. Still though he remains healthy. It's a miracle, many would say.

"Don't you want some?" said Mandy, giving him yet another wide warm smile.

"Yes," he said as he pulled a chair beside her adding "I thought you said you were coming by later tonight, couldn't you just wait?"

"I thought you didn't want to meet me?" she replied, winking at him.

He drew a little smile on his face, snatches the spoon from Mandy's hand, diving it into the thickness and taking a scoop of his favorite ice cream.

Chapter 4

▼

Guy was walking hurridly, he was confused, still thinking of what he has seen, wondering what the hell happened to him. The strange alley, the gate, and the old man; what was all that? Where did it come from? How could someone dream while walking? He wasn't dreaming. He couldn't have been.

Subconsciously, he found himself walking back to his shabby home; he never gave a thought of work.

He stands in front of the apartment building he is living in, it is old and grey. His apartment was on the third floor. He looked up and then walked through the entrance gate.

"Hiya, Kel!" said the doorman; a mid-aged black short family man whose curly, rough hair is a mixture of silver grey and black.

Guy doesn't reply. The day was still young and it was going to be a long one by the looks of it. He wanted to know what time it was. He was not wearing a watch. He never did. He started to stare at passers-by, tilting his head left and right to try and take a look at their watches. It wasn't easy but that was okay. He enjoyed the process.

It's been years since he last wore a watch. No one knows why, even he doesn't know why. When someone would ask him why, he would say it makes him feel more free and relaxed not wearing a watch, though the real reason remains a mystery. Perhaps it's the sense of liberation from the relentless ticking of time and not having to worry about every minute you lose for good. It's the annoyance of not being able to resist glancing at the watch every ten seconds or so. It is the notion of being reminded that your life is getting closer to its end.

Sometimes, though, it could get very annoying even to him. At times when he wants to know the time so bad and he can't find a single watch or clock to know it.

Once, he was going to the movies for a late show. He was already out walking when he decided to go to the eleven o'clock showing but he didn't know what time was it then. He began an arm search and failed and went on to find a watches store to look at the watches displayed in the window but even the store was closed. It took him a long time and he was half an hour late for the movie, but that didn't make him change his mind on wearing watches.

He was still staring at the wrists of passers-by. The look on their faces he finds very amusing.

"It's nine-twenty-five," shouted the doorman. He knew that Guy wouldn't come up to him and ask for the time. No reply from Guy. He thought it would make him feel good to have a drink, so he headed away from the building to go to the nearest place he could find.

"And you are welcome!" yelled the doorman after him, and then shook his head right and left in sympathy.

It was now almost noon and Guy had been sitting on the same chair for the past two hours. He only had one Summer Breeze. The waitress kept coming to him every few minutes asking him politely if he wanted anything else, in an attempt to let him know he should empty the chair now.

He doesn't care. The place wasn't full anyway and it wasn't as if there were people waiting for an empty chair.

"Listen…" he said as he took a quick glance at her nametag "Looky! Losha!!"

"Lucia" she interrupted, with her sweet distant voice.

"Well, Lucia. Stop bugging me or you lose your tip," he said in a stern and serious voice the last time she approached him, she smiled and walked away. Lucia was thin, but her body seemed to fit her. Her dark brown hair was covered with a red cloth and she wore a short skirt and one of those stretch tops with shoulder straps that show your belly button. Guy couldn't help staring at her.

He spent all this time, with that sole drink, looking at people coming in and out of the shop and thinking. He thought of his life and what he ought to do with it, of what has been happening with him and all these years he wasted. And he thought of the dreams he keeps having, the scary and ugly ones, the ones that are more believable yet more unrealistic.

He was a little hungry. A peek into his small black leather wallet suggested he couldn't afford any of the food on the menu. He put his wallet back into the back pocket of his trousers and leaned forward, with his elbows on the table, hands joined together and head pushed against them, back to thinking.

When he looked up again he was met with Lucia's eyes. Observing him. She turned away her sky blue eyes, flicking her hair over her left ear with her soft long thin fingers. He looks at her as she stands beside the bar, holding a tray, her right leg bent a little. She seems elegant, yet weak and vulnerable.

He stood up and walked towards her, feeling heavy with each step he was taking. He felt attracted to her. Suddenly his heart began beating faster and his breathing turned more random, he was nervous. As he got closer to her, just couple of steps away, he felt stupid and silly and regretted even thinking about approaching her. She was still standing, seemingly waiting for him to speak out. What was he thinking?

He stood very close to her, face to face; so close they could feel each other's breaths. Their eyes were wild and full of lust. She was waiting for him to say something. He was waiting for the right words to come out of his mouth; instead he spontaneously reaches into his right pocket, getting out a couple of coins, and offering them to her.

"For the drink." he said, hastily and with a sour voice of regret.

The look on her face was one of great disappointment; she was expecting something else, but why? She asked herself. She was speechless and she was angry and he knew it. He made her feel weaker. He hated himself for that. Could have she been the one? He's been alone too long to know what it felt like to be with someone anymore and that scared him.

Guy turned his back and left the place, disgusted at himself, whispering so softly, hoping that she would hear him, the word "sorry".

Chapter 5

The weather was enhancing. The humidity lower and the air moving more freely, the sun cooling. Signs of autumn, thinks Patrick as he walks side by side with Mandy at the city park. It's fifteen past five in the afternoon. Mandy talked to Pat about the job he should consider applying for, she told him it'll suit him, working three days a week from nine to three. That's it. Six hours, she said. It sounded too good to be true.

"Gives you plenty of time to sleep and wander," she said "and the money is not that bad either!"

He said he would think about it. She knows that after saying that, he means he doesn't want to talk about it further at that moment.

They were walking down the pavement, with grass and trees on both sides. Her arms wrapped around his right arm, her head resting on his shoulder. She is happy when she is with him, she has always been happy. Most of her friends don't know him; she knows that they tell her she'll be better off without him. He is a loser, they'd say, you can do better than that. Mandy wouldn't stand it though. Even her best friend, Christina, hasn't met him.

They've been together for over four years. What she likes about him is that he is moody and delicate and pathetic. Mandy likes to be by his side, to comfort him and to be there for him, she knows what he has been through, he's not spoke about it much with her but she can feel it just by looking at his face. And she likes the sex; not that it's been happening often lately. She doesn't mind. She will wait until he feels better. She's happy with him.

"Look." he says, pointing towards an ice cream stand "Ice-cream. I'll go fetch some."

"Don't worry, I will." and she ran off to the stand before he can even react. "Mandy!" he called after her, but she was already gone. He smiled. He loves her too, but he doesn't show it. He's the kind of man that always keeps his feelings and emotions inside. Not sharing them with anyone.

Now Mandy looks so small, she was waving to him. There looks to be a long queue of children all for ice cream. Patrick is like them, he loves ice cream. He loves the electrifying coldness in his teeth as he takes the first bite. He loves the way it cools his mouth and stomach.

He walks a few steps and takes a look around him. Some kids playing football over there, others running around. A few bikers, a few walkers, and a few joggers. It's been a long time since he was in the park, which isn't the greenest and nicest you'd find; it used to be emptier. Maybe the city changed; maybe it's the weather.

Over to his left, he sees a woman, sitting on the bench, reading a book, and listening to her portable CD player. She looked familiar. She had the kind of face you see in dreams, very real, very familiar, but unrecognizable. She was beautiful. He felt a force attracting him to her. Where have I seen her before? he asked himself. And he found himself walking to her. She was looking down into her book, it seemed like a girlie novel, small and bulky and cute. The weak air of the park played with her dark hair. He stopped close to her and she looked up as she felt his presence. Gently, she removed the headset, put a daisy to mark the page she was reading and gently shut the book. She smiled at him and raised her eyebrows as if asking him what he wants.

"Hello." he said.

"Hello." she said back. Still he can't remember where he saw her before and now he doesn't know why he even came to her. She was wearing a green long sleeved cotton top and dark blue jeans. Just when he was about to speak—even though he wasn't quiet sure what was going to come out of his half-open mouth—he heard someone calling his name.

It was Mandy, jogging her way up to him. "I got your ice-cream."

"Mandy?" said the woman sitting on the bench.

"Chrissy! Hey!" said Mandy in joy. "Do you know each other?"

"No." they both replied.

"Well, Chrissy, this is my Patty. And Honey, this is Chrissy, the one I always tell you about."

"The one that got fired?" he asked, bluntly.

A sudden gloom appeared over both women's faces, one stared at the ground and the other played with her fingers. A short silence.

"Oh, didn't mean to…"

"Never mind." Christina interrupted with a soft smile. "It's ok. And yes, that was me!"

Patrick was confused now. Is that why he thought he knew her? Because she's Mandy's friend. But he never met her before. Mandy handed him his ice cream.

"Would you like to join us?"

"No, Mandy. Thanks. Maybe some other time."

"Are you feeling better? I see you're already starting to enjoy yourself." Mandy said with laughter, trying to joke about it.

"I'm fine. It's okay. Nice to be free!"

Mandy kissed her friend on the cheek and promised that they would "hook up" soon and began to walk away, Patrick stood still for a moment.

"I wish I was a rose," he said with a deep and sincere low voice, that he thought no one else would have heard. But from the look on Christina's face, she heard and she seemed that she wanted to say something.

"Come on Patrick. Let's go." said Mandy from some distance.

Christina and Patrick looked at each other, both puzzled and intrigued, feeling awkward. They felt like there were a lot of things to be said between each other—what though, they didn't know—but they both ignored.

But they also knew deep inside that they would one day meet again.

He's been silent since meeting Chrissy, Mandy ponders, why was that? What happened? His head was downwards. They both glanced and smiled at each other. The sun was beginning to disappear; the sky painted purple and mixed with the orange rays of the setting sun.

"I think we better go back before it gets dark?" He agreed.

When they were a few meters away from his apartment, Mandy still grabbing his arm, he made an announcement.

"I will take that job,"

"Really? That's great!" she said, pleased with herself and with his decision.

She was never pushy, Mandy. Always taking things slowly and easy. When she wants something she doesn't make it look like she won't be happy if she didn't make it happen. She would wait, with her simple smile and easy mood, until you fall into the trap and go for whatever it is that she is looking forward to.

That strategy proved to be successful with her father when she was a little girl. Her father loved her. She loved him as much. When she was twelve, she wanted roller blades. Her father thought it wouldn't be safe for her. She asked once and then after a while, reminded him and that was it. Then she waited, acted normal, behaved well, until finally she got it. She felt great, she felt proud and satisfied. Because she didn't have to cry, or shout, or nag about it. She only smiled.

As they reached the building gate a man passed by, he was smoking. That man reminded Patrick of something. I didn't smoke that fucking cigarette, he said mentally.

"Wait here for a sec, Mandy" as he ran off after that big fat man with the lit cigarette.

"Excuse me, Sir." he called, "Do you have a light?"

The man looked weird. He was short and fat and had some hair on the back and sides of his head. And a moustache like Hitler's!

"Yeah." he replied as he dipped his hand into his coat pocket and offered his silver gas lighter to Patrick. He found it weird that the man was wearing a coat, in this weather.

He lights the cigarette. At last. He feels the smoke run fast through his nose, into his body and into his lungs. Cool and tingling. "Thank you," Patrick said and turned back to his companion.

Mandy stared at him with a confused look, with his cigarette between his fingers, puffing white smoke up into the air through his wet lips. She wanted to comment about the smoking, but she knew better than to ruin the whole day and the rest of the evening over it.

They don't say a thing as they climb up to the apartment and into it. It smells nasty.

"You better get some air freshener darling." she said. He only gave her a frown.

He was thinking now, he's been thinking almost all the time, since meeting Christina. He sits on his untidy bed and thinks even more. About the lighter the fat man had, he's seen that lighter before. Where, oh where? Can't remember. It was embossed with a naked lady wrapped by a big cobra snake. The lady holds a cross in her hand as she screams. He thinks perhaps his father had the same one but his father didn't smoke did he?

"I've seen that lighter before," he said, as if talking to himself. Mandy could barely hear him.

"What did you say?"

It still puzzled him that the man was wearing a coat. There was something leery and garish about him, it annoyed him that he couldn't recall the man's facial features.

"Did that man look funny?"

"What man?" Mandy asked back. She was now inside the bathroom, washing up.

"The man whose lighter I used."

A long pause. No answer. Patrick inhales more smoke from his lit cigarette, already dwindling into a little butt.

"But…" she started, "There wasn't any man Pat!"

What, no man? How come then? She couldn't have *not* seen him?!

"What do you mean?" he asked, extremely puzzled.

"You just walked up there and lit the cigarette. I don't know how or why and I…" as she was speaking, Patrick was already not listening. He was shocked and confused. Suddenly, a thought jumps into his head and he puts his hand into his right jeans pocket and there it was, the silver lighter with the lady and the snake and the cross. He stares at it, observes it with care then throws it on the bed, over the pillow.

"Honey, are you okay?"

"Eh, yeah. I'm…I'm fine." But of course he wasn't fine. Was he going crazy? Was he losing it? Was he dreaming? He inhales more smoke from his cigarette and exhales it through his nose. He feels it filling his lungs, swimming in his head.

"I'm going to take a quick shower okay?"

"Okay."

Patrick looks out the window again, some stars, scattered across the sky, began to materialize, some of them brighter than others. His hands were joined. He thinks maybe it's time for him to shake it off and join the normality of people around him. Maybe it's time to get a job and get a life. But how could he simply dismiss what he had witnessed. Where did that fat man come from? Damn it, what was that?

Slowly, he begins to feel movement on the bed. Must be Mandy, shower over so soon? He looks behind him and there, right in front of his eyes, on his own bed, was the naked lady, wrapped with the big cobra snake.

He froze. Not moving a muscle. Not even breathing.

They were alive and they were big. His eyes opened wide.

"That's impossible, he whispered, "Can't be real!" He wanted to run off, to call for Mandy. But he couldn't.

The lady was of fine figure. She was horny. Her face was pure and simple with beautiful big blue eyes. Her hair was long and ran down to her hips and was as yellow and bright as the shining noon sun. Her breasts were big and round and her nipples were smooth and the color of brown bread. Her hips were wide. Her stomach was flat. Her thighs were fat and her legs were long with a snow-white complexion.

The big dark-skinned snake was wrapping around her, moving maliciously over the lady's sexy body. Now the room was all black. Nothing was familiar to Patrick's eyes anymore. There was but the woman and snake on the bed, the sheets had turned red. At the beginning he was afraid, but now, surprisingly to himself, this lady aroused him. He felt he wanted to be with her, he felt he wanted to fuck her. He was astonished for a mere second to see himself naked as well. He reached out his hand slowly and gently and touched her thigh.

Just as he placed his hand over her body he felt comfort and safe. It was a confusing and frustrating feeling. Slowly he moved his hand upwards, touching her thigh, up to her hip, stomach, breast, and neck and on to her face. He touched her fat rich lips with his finger; she began to moan to his touch.

The snake snapped. It looked angry and ready to attack, but Patrick was not afraid. He wanted her, that was all that was in his head. He wanted her so bad nothing was going to stop him, not even the big cobra snake around her.

He could feel the snake's skin, grouchy and glittering, slithering over his. Almost feeling like greased rubber. He brings up his head against hers. He was about to kiss her. He can't wait to press his lips against hers. Before he shut his eyes to do so, he looked straight into her eyes. She was looking straight back at him with those wild strong blue eyes. But there was something wrong. Something unsafe. He felt danger from her eyes. There was something behind these beautiful perfect blue eyes. It was as if her eyes were trying to tell him something, trying to warn him of the danger…but what danger? He felt cold metal pressed against his arm. It was the cross the lady was holding. It was so cold; he felt his arm freezing, burning bitterly. It was painful.

He closed his eyes and let out a gruesome scream.

"What? What's wrong?" said Mandy as she stormed into the room, naked of but for a little towel and soaking wet.

He grabbed his left arm, where the lady pressed her cross, it pained him much. Mandy hurried to him.

"Let me see that." she demanded. "Hey, you didn't tell me you had a tattoo. You scared the hell out of me. When did you get it?" she asked, examining the drawing.

"Just now." he said, taking a difficult deep breathe "Just now." he said again with a face of a man who saw the death of God, as tears fell down the edge of his horrified eyes.

Chapter 6

He was sitting on his chair, watching television. He's been watching one of those cheap action B-movies where you could predict every move and every line, and know the outcome from the first scene. You are always one step ahead of it. Goes something like this: A decent cop facing a lot of problems, divorced, middle aged, having a bad run fighting crime. A mob is going around town killing people and asking for trouble for no reason but it would very likely involve drugs. The bad cop is on to them. Of course his father was a cop too and he was killed in the line of duty. His wife wants to take their only child (most probably a girl) away from him. He is broke and drunkard.

In the end he shoots all the bad guys. Including the boss who turns out to be the one who killed his father. It happened when the cop caught him alone. He surrenders and tells him "Kill me, come on do it, avenge your father." but of course the troubled cop doesn't kill him because he is honest in his job and he would leave the bad guy to "rot in prison".

So he turns his back away, the bad guy then draws a little hand gun from his socks and before he knows it he gets a bullet into his forehead from our quick and intelligent hero-cop. Oh, and our hero would also fall in love with the woman who was forced into the criminal acts of the mob.

The end.

What a story! What a crap!

So Guy sits, and sits, watching, eyes half closed, eating a stale tuna sandwich and drinking a soda.

He'd been to see some of his old friends that afternoon, something he doesn't enjoy much doing but that it does him some good. It was fine though, just fine.

It's not like before, hanging around with friends. It's different now. They all seemed to lead a normal good life, unlike him, which made him feel more of an outcast than ever before.

One, a taunting big-chested man, was working in a bank; another, tall and thin and geeky, was working in a computer company.

"So what are you doing now Kelton?" One long forgotten friend asked him.

"Nothing," he replied, "I am doing nothing."

Today, he did not go to work and he was thinking he would not go tomorrow and they day after. Sick of being treated like a slave and realizing there was no point in what he does anyway. Guy was working in a drug store. He moved boxes and carried them around the store.

"Oh well, maybe I'm being punished for something? Maybe I am punishing myself?" he said in a low voice, talking to himself, as he drank up the soda "Penance…They call it penance. I'll drink to that!"

Then, unusually, sleepiness crept into him and within minutes he was sleeping like a dead horse. It was only around seven in the evening! An unusual time to nap. But it's the only time that he could sleep as easily as he would ever dream of, unfortunately though, it would always last for a short time. He would just sit on the couch, relax, a few minutes would pass and bam, he's asleep.

But his eyes were opened quickly, as a matter of fact, they were opened after what he felt was a fraction of a second, from closing them to sleep.

The TV was still on but now the picture was unfocused and fuzzy. He can't make anything out of it from the first look. He hears nothing. Except the sound of quietness and silence. Oh yes, silence does make a sound; it's that annoying ever-lasting buzz that drives you insane. But this time it was louder, too loud to be able to concentrate on the TV; he wanted to know what was on it. What this fuzzy picture was.

Guy doesn't know for sure if he was asleep or awake. When he closed his eyes, was it just another blink, or was it the final close before drifting into sleep? Now the picture on the TV was starting to clear bit by bit. He could see two figures, human figures, a man and a woman. He concentrates more and more on the screen, which was glowing with its grey, blue rays, casting itself over him and around him. He realizes that the sound of the silence ceased. How come? he thought. He hears nothing, absolutely nothing, for the very first time in his life. Not even his heartbeats and his breath. He hears nothing at all.

At that quiet second he also realised that he cannot move himself, not his legs, not his hands, not his head, not even his eyes. He was stiff as a stone. The picture was finally clear, in it were two people, strange to Guy, but not to each other.

They both wore a long white robe, covering all their body except their heads. They were talking. It looked like an episode of some soap/sci-fi opera, he thought. It didn't make sense

It seemed to go on for some time and Guy couldn't understand what they were saying. He felt a shudder and then coldness as they, the man and the woman, stared at him with eyes of fire and of ice. They stared at him and he couldn't do anything but stare back. Their faces, he cannot focus on. The woman spoke. She said with a voice that sounded like the hiss of a thousand cats "Join us Guy Kelton. Join us before it's too late. Do not let go."

He stiffened even more, fear consuming him, enveloping him. What's going on? Oh, God. Not again. It was happening to him again. He was in the weird and scary world of the dreaming.

Guy decided then to wake up. He did.

The movie was still on. Our hero cop was now chasing the bad guy to kill him in the final scene. Guy looks to his left and the sandwich and soda can were still there. He quenches the sudden thirst with the rest of the soda. He pulled his body away from the chair and stood up; just to make sure everything was back to normal.

"I hope I'm not going crazy."

The next morning, just after ten o'clock, Guy's phone rang. It was his boss from work, asking if he was coming in today. No, he wasn't. The boss asked why? He said because he wanted to rest and he would like it if no one bothered him anymore. The boss said he should come back to work whenever he's feeling better. Guy said if I ever got better and hung up the phone. He wondered, just like he had so many time before, why his boss didn't get mad at him. He never did. Guy didn't know if it was because the boss wasn't the type to get ratty or if he was just way too nice. He couldn't see him being either.

He threw his head on the pillow and regretted not telling him to go to hell with his stupid job. But something prevented him from doing such a thing, the same thing that controls all of his decisions; the unquestioned force that drives us to the unknown eventual destinations we stumble to.

"I will go to the market this morning," he said to himself.

He got up, had a quick hot cup of black coffee, no sugar, no milk, just plain black coffee, dressed and walked out of his own world into the outer foreign world. No more routine. No more autopilot mode. Break the cycle.

As he walked down the stairs, he heard people moving and talking, as he passed their apartment doors. One particular apartment though has always been silent, ever since Guy moved into the building. He has never heard or seen the people living inside this apartment, on the second floor. The other day, he asked the doorman about them. He said he saw only the man who paid the rent, "He was an old man," he told Guy, "In his late sixties probably. He paid two years upfront, I don't know were da hell he came up with dat kinda moolah."

So, as he reached that door, he stood for a minute, in silence, trying to listen to anything from within this place. But he was startled by the scream of a woman, shouting at her son perhaps.

It was Mrs. Jacker. Her husband died a year ago and now she is raising the children on her own, she is too ugly for any other man to want to marry her now. How on earth Mr. Jacker married her in the first place was anyone's guess, she was as ugly as a monkey and as loud as a donkey.

Mr. Jacker was found in an alley behind the building, stabbed and electrocuted. It was a bizarre incident. The police didn't bother with his case. At first they said it was a suicide, and then they said they don't know for sure, and then they said it was an accident and then they forgot about it.

Guy continued his descent, with each step he took down the stairs a different sound popped, and Mrs. Jacker was still shouting at her children.

The sun was as bright as it always been during the summer, though Guy can see some scattered dots of clouds. Strange, he thought, and stranger was having a dry cool breeze on a day like this. It was the last week of August, but still it was summer.

The market was few blocks away from where he lived. He walked steadily, looking down as usual, he don't want his eyes in contact with any other person because he knows if he did, he will only see hatred and disgust and boredom and sadness and despair in the people's eyes, or perhaps they will see it in his eyes.

Some bad music drew his attention; it was coming from a little girl down the street playing the harmonica. It was obvious she didn't have a clue how to play it; she was very bad at it. Guy approached her and stood in front of her. She was wearing a little white dress and a wide straw hat. She was pale and looked ill. She was about five years old. There was a white handkerchief placed at her feet with only two small coins. Guy thought she might as well have placed them herself.

He bent his legs so that he could be in direct contact with her eyes. She stopped playing her awful tune and looked back at him. He saw the most innocent and lost pair of eyes he'd ever seen in his life.

"What's your name?" he asked.

She just looked at him with a grin.

"I'm called Guy," he said "Here, let me help you with that." He stretched out his hand to her. The girl looked at him inquisitively. She looked around her before reluctantly giving him the shiny instrument. He placed it on his lips, wrapped his hands about it and started playing a tune he had learnt many years ago, he even surprised himself how good he could play it.

When he was younger, his mother gave him a silver harmonica with a guidebook and he taught himself and he was good at it. Then he lost the harmonica, or pretended he lost it because everyone thought he was annoying and didn't want to listen to him, at least his father was clear about that.

The girl looked up at him as he stood playing beside her. An old woman passed by, throwing some money onto the white handkerchief on the ground and gave the child some candy she had in her little purse and smiled at them.

"Stop it!" said the little girl, after the woman left, "I said stop it!" This time louder.

"Why? Don't you like my music?" asked Guy smiling. He was starting to enjoy it. It freed him of his miseries for a while.

They stood silent side by side for a moment before the girl spoke again. "My father will come soon and he would not appreciate you being here, doing this."

"Oh. Right. I apologize." He wanted to ask why, but preferred not to.

"You play nice music." She told him, looking down at her little feet.

"Well, that is very nice of you to say little one." he waved his hand to her and turned around, ruefully walking away, saying in a sorrowful whisper "You do too,"

"Angela," she quietly muttered. "That's what I am called."

He smiled, feeling a pinch in his heart, as he went along without looking back.

The market was full of people of all kinds and levels. Vendors were shouting out their prices and offers at passers-by, hoping to sell something fast. This was the peak time for the market, and yet still, even though you see many people around, they weren't buying much.

Guy walked in the center of the street, flanked by small shops and stands where vendors and traders sell vegetables, fruits and all sort of exotic foods and spices. The ground was wet. He stops in the middle of the street, looks to his left, looks to his right and then down to the ground, he was standing in a little puddle of water, he sees his reflection. It had a sad face. A big shoulder of a big muscular man bumped into him. Rambo just shot a torrid look at Guy without uttering a word. Guy didn't bother about him. People are like that here, rude and lackadaisical.

Guy turned his head toward a vendor selling all sorts of fruits. His mouth was watering. The old lady, sitting behind her stall, squinted at him, her eyes barely visible on her crumpled face. She wore a thin cloth as a headscarf to cover her wispy white hair. Guy picked a green apple and paid the old woman for it.

"God bless you son." she said, her raspy voice seemed to animate her worn face as she spoke "If you don't mind me saying son, you look like someone who has just lost all that he is living for. Just smile it off darling,"

"Believe me, ma'am what I lost does not mean anything to me," he said, referring to his job. She smiled at him. Guy nodded and walked away, biting at the green skin of the apple, crunching its white juicy gut with his teeth.

Some clouds began to design the sky with snow-white-cotton-like shapes. It's been a long while since the last time there were such clouds in the sky. Guy looked up at them and whished he could fly up there and touch them with his fingertips, maybe even eat them. Always wondered how would clouds taste, they must taste lovely he thought to himself and giggled and continued his walk into the crowds of people in the market, eating his apple and enjoying the surprisingly improving weather.

Maybe it will be good now, he told himself, maybe life will finally smile at me, maybe the old lady was right and I should just smile it all off, and the hell with the world.

Chapter 7

Patrick Roymint still doesn't know why he said he'd take that driver job at Mandy's company a week ago. Was it because he was running out of money? Or because he felt he should straighten up his life style and be normal? Or because he wanted to keep Mandy happy?

He was driving the company's van to deliver a package to another company. It's his first errand and his first day at work. How stupid, he thought, why not use DHL for their fucking deliveries.

He drove down the main street away from the city center. He had to take this package to some bloke in a small restaurant in the poorest neighborhood of the town, an area called Ashbed. It wasn't a long drive. He switched on the radio, listened to music and looked at the people, the cars, the buildings and neighborhoods he passed by with strange eyes. He hadn't been around to different parts of town for a long time, but it all looks the same to him.

There would come a day where every man wakes up and realises that he is no more than just a lone soul amongst billions of souls, on a planet in the middle of a solar system that is only one of millions of other systems in a galaxy placed in the vast ocean of endless balkiness of millions of other galaxies, surrounded by stars a million times bigger than the sun and some even bigger then a galaxy…and then you would think how surreal all of this is and you would wonder and you would be afraid of this notion.

It is pretty scary to be such a little thing in such big a place.

That's how he was feeling right then. It was that sort of thinking that helped Patrick get over the loss of his family, made him immune from the harshness of life and reality.

An old empty building caught his attention on the left hand side as he neared Ashbed. It was the rescue station his father was headquartered in, now all forlorn and derelict. Flashes of old memories began to surface as he stopped at the red light near the station, barely standing, alone, half wrecked, half broken. It looked like a ghost house. Haunted by the souls of the people who served for years, trying to save other people who were complete strangers to them.

Patrick remembers the rare occasions when his father would bring him in to show him the different tools and equipment they used in their missions—he loved the chopper, although he never got the opportunity to go for a ride in it. He would feel like he was the happiest and luckiest kid in the whole world, to have a brave and kind father like that. He found himself reliving one particular memory, that one day when his father took him to work for the first time. He was so excited.

That Monday morning, which coincided with little Pat's sixth birthday, his father's booming voice broke Patrick's sleep.

"Are you ready for some action Patty boy?"

Patrick, hearing this, jumped off of his bed and ran to the bathroom to wash up and get ready. It took him less than a minute! His mother wasn't very happy about it and wished that her son could get ready just as fast on a school morning!

Just as they arrived at the station an emergency call was made and everything turned sour. Patrick didn't even get a chance to look round. People were running around like mad—one man almost knocked him over—yelling and shouting at each other. His father came to him and said with a worrying small voice "Sorry kiddo, Daddy got to go save some lives!" Patrick understood that his daddy had to go but it still left him disappointed and angry.

"I promise I'll be back before you know it son and we'll do a tour for you, you just stay here and don't move." He told him, patting his son on both his shoulders.

Patrick sat on a small chair on the corner of his father's office and did nothing; he waited and waited and waited; for three hours he sat on that chair, never moving, anticipating the return of his hero father.

But when he did return, his father was very upset, angry and devastated. They were very close to losing someone because of a misjudgment he made. It could have proven a fatal mistake, but fortunately the rescuers recovered and managed to get to the victim in time.

"What happened dad? Can we go see the chopper now?" asked young Pat innocently. His father was in no mood for all of that now. The promise was forgotten and broken.

Pat remembers how his father's face looked that moment, so wicked and red and pathetic. He never forgot that face, would never forget it, especially that it was the same face that his father wore, one year later, after returning from his mothers' and sisters' rescue operation: disappointed and angry and sad.

It was loud horns and men's cursing that brought Patrick's attention back to the road, the light was green, he kicked in the accelerator and sped ahead.

"I am as pathetic as you are, Dad," he said bitterly.

In another five minutes, Patrick reached the place where he was supposed to hand the package. The streets were dirty and the air was filled with the smell of human waste. The restaurant was located in a three-storey building. It looked okay for a poor neighborhood, he thought.

He parked his van on the side of the pavement and walked the few meters to the restaurant. It was empty of people; the whole area seemed breathless. A few creepy crawlers would appear for a moment and then disappear into the dark alleys and wet streets. A sudden feel of insecurity crept into Patrick's mind, his body shuddering from the heavy air. The restaurant door was closed. A quick peek through the window offered nothing but empty chairs and tables and dark rooms.

"Hello!" he yelled through the door and knocked with the side of his fist on it a few times, there was no answer.

As he turned his back, rubbing his forehead, he heard a knock on the window. A thin man with long hair and a big beard was gesturing to him to go in from the back door. It was midday, shouldn't the restaurant be bustling with people for lunch? Suspicion grew further with Patrick, but he kept assuring himself and putting it down to nerves on the first day.

The alley was filled with rubbish and old dirty newspapers. Rats and rodents roamed freely. As he stood in front of the metal back door, a movement caught his attention. It was a homeless old man, sitting near the rubbish container. His clothes were torn. He wrapped an old cloth around his head. His white beard was colored with soot. He was thin and his face was nothing but a shapeless skull.

The door opened. A rough voice invited him to get in. He walked behind the thin man over to an office.

"Wait here," ordered the man, raising his right hand palm against Patrick's face. He looked around. A strong filthy smell was making him feel a bit dizzy. He could see two figures through the blurred window of the office, arguing about something. He decided he should sit on the lone chair placed across the hall but as he neared it, a disgusting scene made him sick to the stomach. There was a huge black rodent feeding on a little dead mouse, under the chair.

The thin man invited him into the office. The look in the man's eyes did not give much comfort to Patrick.

He sensed evil in them.

The office he entered was a total contrast to the hall and outside. Its air was fresh and filled with incense, the floor and the furniture were all clean and spotless and the room was as bright as the noon sun.

"Is that our stuff?" the big bald man with black sunglasses said to Patrick as he puffed out smoke off his Cuban cigar. The mob-boss-like man sat behind a big desk, on a leather armchair, wearing expensive jewelry and designer clothes. His voice was ragged.

"I-I guess so," replied the delivery boy, "You will have to sign here." He couldn't help noticing that man's bad teeth. They were obscene and hideous. Some were black as coal and others as yellow as rotten milk. The big man could feel Patrick's eyes almost popping out staring at those teeth. It's the cigars probably, he thought.

The thin man was standing near the door examining Patrick with fixed eyes.

"I know what I have to do," growled the big man as his muscles flexed when he reached for the package, "but do you know what you have to do, dog?" There was a menacing grin on his face.

Patrick didn't know what he meant. What was all this about? He wondered to himself. Only now, Patrick remembered what his boss at work had told him.

"Don't ask about anything, don't say anything and don't look at anything," he told him, but why? Said Patrick.

"All you have to do is deliver the package and leave," Patrick never even asked what was in that package. Mandy had told him it would all be foodstuff or business papers that he would deliver.

As Patrick walked out the door, drawing a cigarette from his Camel pack, he felt an urge to go to the toilet. Apparently, the thin man forgot to shut the door after him, so he went in again to ask for a place to pee. The office door was ajar. He could hear three voices. He could recognize the big man and the thin man', the third was unrecognizable. He tiptoed across the hall, getting closer and closer. He was curious but realized that if he got any closer he might get caught. He then heard some sniffing and something about "The good stuff"!

A quick mind refreshing made him remember seeing some needles on the floor of that office as well as some white powder on the coffee table that looked like Coffee-Mate to him.

It was drugs they were talking about and it was drugs that he had delivered to them. It must have been. He didn't know what to do. Should he inform the police? Of course he should. But maybe he should tell Mandy first; she would know what to do.

Fuck! What am I going to do?

Shaken by this discovery, Patrick forgot about his urges and left the place in a hurry. Soon enough, he was already in his van heading as far from this place as he could. He wanted to think, but couldn't. The traffic was starting to soar by now.

"I need a break," he announced to himself.

It was cloudy, a truly early autumn day with a cool soft breeze. A few brown leaves dribbling on the ground. Patrick could have enjoyed the day much better if it weren't for what he had just witnessed.

He would have liked to go out on a bike, just like when he was a teenager, maybe go to a coffee shop, go around the mall, and sit a while at the park, read a book. It would have been a perfect day, but instead here he was, sitting on a bench in front of Capital Hall in the city center, contemplating.

But he didn't actually see anything, did he? He just presumed it; it was just a collective assumption. Maybe they were talking about some foodstuff, smelling it and tasting it, like…like cinnamon! But no, no, that can't be. The way they looked, the way they moved, and the place they were in. It all adds up doesn't it? It could only mean one thing. But why would he care anyway?

By that point he was a nervous wreck, he wanted to calm down and forget about all this, to start the day over.

Ah! A cigarette would do the trick. He forgot the one he had in his hand as he got out of that office. He pulled out another one now and lit it up with his lighter, the silver one with the snake and the naked woman and the cross. Every time he used it, it reminded him of what happened that evening, the tattoo always itching and burning cold.

He had started cutting down ever since, but simply couldn't contemplate quitting the habit completely. He looked down at it, flipped it over and put it back into his pocket. The first puff was fine, so fine he felt his chest opening, he felt the tingling of the smoke in his lungs and after he exhaled the smoke, something very amusing happened, he felt a change in him.

And he suddenly realised he does not want to ever smoke another cigarette for the rest of his life.

Chapter 8

▼

Life is like a dream. It's unpredictable, full of surprises and feelings of surrealism.

Or so Christina Heywood believes. She is still jobless and liking it. Today she sits in her bedroom listening to her old music records and looking at old photographs, recalling the sweet memories of the past, when she and Mandy would spend more times together, talking, laughing and rejoicing.

There was a time, when Christina was just sixteen, when all she cared about was going to the theater to watch old films and shopping at the few little charity shops and reading a classic in the park. She would go out every Thursday morning to the Morning Market with Mandy, then to the catch the noon screening and go to the park afterwards to enjoy the sunshine and the smell of grass in spring.

Summer in Okay is the longest of seasons. The heat is so hard to beat, leaving the body so weary, feeling exhausted and sleepy all the time. Christina didn't mind the sun of course; she actually likes lying under it when it's nicely warm, when you can feel the sunrays on your skin, warming your blood.

"It's like enlightening the insides of my body. Saturating it with the sun's rays." she told Mandy one hot June day that seems so far away now, as if it had happened in a different lifetime.

She was looking at a photo of her and her friend. They were at the park, Mandy sitting under a big tree shielding herself with its shade from the hot sunshine, and Christina lying in the middle of the grass, soaking up the sun. Her mother was sitting on a near-by bench talking to whomever she thought she knew, or did know, who happened to be passing by. Once every few minutes she would look at her young daughter to check on her, making sure no one was bothering her. She wouldn't let any boy come near her, not without her supervision. Her mother was very protective, too protective, Christina would confess, protective to the point of embarrassment.

She remembers that day well. She has always had a good memory. She remembers what she had told Mandy as she lay on that grass, her eyes shut as the sun cast its bright hot rays on her, her arms stretched to her sides. Mandy was complaining about how hot it was.

"I don't hate being hot…its good to be warm, sometimes. And I don't hate being cold either," she dreamily began, "I love winter and I love summer. I love spring and I love autumn. I love it when it's sunny and love it when it's cloudy. To me, the sun is as beautiful as the moon.

"I love mountains and I love the beach. I love being dry and I love being wet. Rain, snow, grass, trees, dead leaves. I love them all. I love the smell of the ocean, and the smell of the streets after rain. And sand. And stars. Love those too. I love the feeling of having the sun to my face. When I close my eyes and feel its warmth over my eyelids, seeing it go brightly red.

"I love colors, all of them. The true colors; red, green, blue, black, purple, yellow, brown, orange, white. I love looking at photos and remembering certain moments. But most of all, I love memories and how they make me feel."

As Christina was reliving that moment, the record player stopped, its final track fading into the ether. She flicked through her stack of records and picked up The Supremes.

Christina Heywood started thinking about her ex-boyfriend. He was handsome and a good man. His name was Aaron Minister. They'd known each other for almost two years. Before meeting him Christina had no interest in boys. She and Aaron dated and that was it. Went out shopping, to movies, lunches and dinners, spent a lot of time together. But all of Aaron's efforts to get closer to Christina failed. She would not let him. They kissed and caressed, occasionally, but she would never make love to him. She was shy. But it wasn't just that, there was a deeper cause for it that she had always refused to accept.

She regrets how it ended. He loved her and cared for her and she loved him and cared for him just as much in return, or at least she thought she did. They had a great time together, but Aaron was hoping to take their relationship to the next level, to progress.

One day, two weeks before she was sacked from her job, on a calm and sticky night, Aaron sat beside her on the brown-leathered couch in his apartment. She didn't go often to his place but he managed to convince her that night. They sat there in silence for an awkward moment before he finally asked her if she loved him or not. She said of course she did.

"Then why won't you let me get closer to you?' She did not answer. She just looked down and played with her fingers just like a child would do.

After a while, he leaned toward her, slid his hand under her chin, then ran his long fingers through her coffee-colored hair and kissed her soft lips. When he attempted slowly to undress her she felt terrible and was very uncomfortable. Her heart beat faster and she grew nervous as something told her that what she was about to do was wrong. She backed off and asked him to leave her alone. He sighed and got upset.

"I'm sorry," he said, shaking his head "But I can't go on like this," That was all he said. Christina started crying and left the apartment.

Two days later she found out that Aaron, on that same night, slept with another woman. He never called her and she never wanted to hear from him. She cried bitterly though, she shed rivers of tears, not because she had lost a good man and destroyed their love, but because she thought she was pathetic. She still thinks she is.

A look outside the window of Christina's room suggested that the day was beginning to fade out, the sun dropping lower and becoming weaker. She had spent all the morning hours at her room. Wonder what mother is up to? She asked herself.

Living with her mother wasn't the ideal choice for Christina, but it was the only choice. Her mother, Natalie, was a very old woman, and very sick. The doctor had given her a couple of months to live.

"I'm afraid you ain't got much time left Mrs. Heywood, I'm sorry to say, there's nothing we can do," Dr West had told them, a couple of months ago, when Christina took her reluctant mother for a check-up.

Dr West was one of the very few specialized doctors in town. It seemed that all doctors fled Okay in search for a better career. He came to the town thirteen years ago with a young pregnant wife. No one knew exactly where he was from; they could barely afford to appreciate him being there.

"It's Statman," snapped the old woman. "The name is Statman," ignoring the doctor, in a voice as fragile as silk. She never visited the doctor again.

She knew therapy would cost a fortune and it probably wouldn't work, especially here in the shitty town of abandonment. The way she saw it, she preferred spending the money on enjoying herself before dying than in the miserable company of doctors and nurses.

Natalie always liked to be called by her maiden name, especially after her husband, Frank Heywood, left one day to work and never came back.

"Got loads to do today honey," he said on a rainy winter day, "Reckon I'll be late," picking up his raincoat and helmet.

He used to work as a construction supervisor. Christina was five when he left. She saw him running to his car, under the pouring rain, from her tight little room window, as sharp drops of rain smashed against the thick glass. As he prepared to get in, he stood for a moment and looked at the house. It wasn't a big house, their house, but it was a cozy one. It was painted beige. He shook his head, bent into the car and drove away. Just before he did, Christina thought she saw him wipe his face. She likes to think that it was a tear but it might easily been the rain.

That was the last Christina saw of her Dad.

Blood was smattered all over the old colorful Persian rug and on the wooden tiles. It was Natalie's blood. She was coughing out her own blood. She was coughing so hard that Christina, still up in her bedroom listening to her music, felt the whole house shaking.

Christina ran down the stairs like crazy, jumping two or three steps at a time. As she ran down the stairs, many thoughts occurred to her, flashing so fast in her mind. It was almost like a dream. What will she do? Who should she call? How would she arrange the funeral? Who would shed tears over her mother but herself?

Natalie insisted on not going to the hospital; she said they would not do her any good, besides she knew she was going to die, there and then. It was her time.

Christina lay beside her on the bed, under the puffy lemon quilt. Her mother was resting, still and breathless, eternally. It was horrible. Seeing her own mother die in front of her eyes, in her hands. Time seemed to have stopped. Everything was slow. Christina felt as if she was separated from the reality of the world surrounding her. She sobbed, silently, tears running pure and true, honest and innocent, until her eyes turned red. She started sweating. Her heart beating slowly, her hands trembling as she held her mother's head within them. Christina's soul ached. The whole affair was too hard and difficult to comprehend and accept, even though she knew that her mother's time was up and that there was no stopping the course of nature. That did not ease the pain, nor softened the blow.

She looked at her mother, the once socially-active-and-loving-house wife, with sympathy. It was like watching a very important part of your body, something precious, being ripped apart from you, very, very slowly, hurting you, bleeding you, scaring you, forever.

Natalie knew she was pathetic before she died. She didn't want to become a burden to anyone and she didn't want to die alone in hospital. That's why she was strongly against being put into a care-home or hospitalized. She didn't want to face the eyes of strangers staring at her with pity and brevity.

"Don't worry honey. I loved you. Always have. Always will," her mother said on the bed of death, her tongue turning red with blood.

"Don't have vanity…and you will keep your sanity"

A long hiss came out with the last word she uttered, the sound of the last breath, escaping the body, the spirit leaving the mind. Those were the last words to come out of her, almost an hour ago now.

Christina was still shattered and submerged in pain and grief, still thinking and wondering what her mother meant by those words. It struck her even deeper when she suddenly realized that she was now completely alone; no one to love and care for, no one to keep an eye on, no one to embrace, at a time like this.

"Well, mother," whimpered Christina to her dead mother, "Here I am at last, and in the position I never wanted to be." Her voice was full of agony. She looked at her mother's corpse with watery eyes and sighed,

"Alone,"

Chapter 9

It was raining the following week, on the day of the funeral, which was, by all standards, a pretty quick one; very subdued. Everything happened so fast—The prayers, the awkward moment of silence, the lowering of the casket, all done in mechanic motion, subtle and sublime.

A few people were scattered around the burial session. There stood Christina, holding a beautiful white lily in one hand, and beside her stood her friend Mandy. There were also a couple of neighbors, one passer-by and an uncle who she had not seen for four years.

Patrick hadn't come. Even though Mandy thought he should have.

The Council Cemetery, located in the backdrop of Kingland, was messy. Grass patches were scattered across the land. Most of it seemed to have not been irrigated for a long time. It was thirsty, and it flourished with the taste of sweet rainwater as it dripped from the grey sky. Of course the sun made it's presence felt as well, as it beamed down warm pale rays through the tight holes of the darkened grey clouds, which covered the sky like a duvet.

After her mother died, Christina had managed to gather enough strength to call an ambulance; she then called her uncle who had a friend whose brother was an undertaker.

She had been surprisingly calm then, but now as they lowered the casket into the grave, Christina's cries were hard and strong. She gasped frequently and she mourned bitterly. Mandy squeezed her best friends' hand firmly with one hand as a gesture of support. Letting her know that she's right there beside here. The other hand she placed over Christina's shoulder. Mandy, try as she may, couldn't keep from crying at the sight of her best friend in such distress and pitiful agony. She kept squeezing Christina's hand, pulling her closer, and embracing her.

Several minutes passed, before Christina raised her head and looked behind to her right, noticing a young man standing there, under the rain, which now started to phase out to just a drizzle. It was Patrick. She recognized him even though he wore a head cap and sunshades. He waited until the ceremony was over to approach her. By now the rain fully stopped and the holes in the cloud widened, letting more of those warm sunrays pass through. Christina thought she never seen more beautiful weather, than in that one moment. It was perfect. The wet grass looked lively and the autumn breeze mixed wonderfully with the warmth of the sun. She found a great comfort in the simple beauty of the weather, something she has always admired and worshipped.

Patrick didn't say anything. He stood in front of her, leaned toward her and kissed her forehead. His eyes, behind the sunshades, were sincere and sad. He wanted her to see them, but at the same time he thought that if she did, she would not realize it. He wanted to say sorry, but he reckoned it would be inappropriate. He hated saying sorry in situations like these.

Instead, he simply took off his sunshades to reveal the most beautiful eyes Christina had ever seen. He stared into those watery familiar eyes of hers and she stared back, caught in the heat of the moment, with Mandy staying behind them looking down as if she was an intruder between two lovers, surprised at Patrick's presence.

There was no need for words, and it was obvious that both of them were glad.

A figure approached them then. They all felt it and turned to face it. It was the unknown passer-by; they were surprised by his sudden approach. The stranger stood, motionless. Mandy thought he was looking straight at Patrick, she was right. Patrick looked at the strange man with repelling eyes, full of condemnation and fire. The stranger looked back with disturbing eyes.

The two women were strangers to Guy, though one of them seemed vaguely familiar. After a stretched few seconds, the silence was broken.

"We need to talk, you and I," said the stranger.

"We do?"

"Something's happening. I don't know what it is. It's hard to talk about. But I know it concerns both of us," the stranger paused. Patrick said nothing. Then the stranger added: "See you tonight at the Marco's Bar?"

Patrick nodded.

Christina and Mandy looked at the stranger—he was frumpy, and had an intimidating demeanor—and then at Patrick in bewilderment and shock. The stranger nodded at the ladies then left the cemetery.

He's been at the bar for the last hour. The place was poorly lit. Several men and women were scattered all across the barn-like bar. A band of five black men were playing some decent blues music in the background. They wore tuxedos. One of them looked like Ray Charles.

Guy could hear a drunkard cursing his own luck, moaning about his wife who ran away with his sister; another was loudly celebrating his win at a snooker game with his folk. Marco's was filled with misery, irony and blasphemy and a thick, tight air of smoke and booze. It was a small bar, so small that even though it wasn't packed with people, it made Guy feel claustrophobic.

He was getting nervous and impatient as it dawned at him that he had not set a time for the meeting. He was wondering why he went up to that man—who reminded him of someone he might have known as a kid—at the funeral in the first place, and why he wanted to meet him.

Guy scanned the room for a clock. He found one hanging on the wall. It marked three minutes after midnight. He drank up his pint in one full gulp. As he put the mug down he realized that his guest has arrived. Patrick said, "Well, what is it you want. I am not afraid of you, you know?"

Guy looked at him with a puzzled expression on his face.

"I know that you know that I saw what you didn't want me to see but I did. So spill it."

Guy seemed confused. He knows what it's happening to him, he thought. That's strange. How could he?

"Please sit. I am called Guy. You?"

"I think you know that already, don't you?" But from the look at Guy's face, Patrick realized he didn't.

"Right. I'm Patrick," he muttered.

Both men didn't know what to say next. There were no handshakes. Patrick sat down beside Guy on a little bar stool against a window screen, facing the street.

"Well, it seems that we are both in the same situation. But please, tell me what *you* saw?" said Guy, as he motioned for the bartender for another round.

Patrick thought about the incident when he delivered the package to the restaurant, trying to remember the details. He felt as if he knew that man, there was something familiar about him. It didn't occur to him to question why he was there.

"I didn't want to see anything. I just had to come back and it just popped out in front of me as I was..." he struggled with words.

"Yeah. I know," interrupted Guy, "that's how it started with me too. You see, I was going to work one day and then all of a sudden I was someplace that I didn't want to be and," now he was struggling with words. "It was just very bizarre and scary!"

The waitress came up with two pints and placed them in front of the two men. She was chubby and vulgar and was aggressively chewing bubble gum.

Both men fell speechless for a minute or two as they tried to recollect their thoughts, each lost and confused, trying to make sense of this situation.

Patrick failed to come to a conclusion and was starting to quiver from the smell of smoke. He thought he should have a cigarette; the urge was consuming. He fought it and concentrated on what was on hand.

"So what's the score?" he asked.

"What do you think, Patrick?"

After a moment of hesitation he said "I just want to live normally. Stay out of trouble,"

Guy closed his eyes, sighed and then looked ahead. "I'm afraid it's not that simple," he said. Tension was building up.

They sat silently, listening to the music, facing the street through the large window, when a peculiar young boy walking on the other side of the road caught their attention.

The boy was limping awkwardly and sharply, his limp head was tilting in all directions as he moved. Guy and Patrick stared at him, lost in that strange moment. The boy stood there in the middle of the road as the two men froze still, forgetting about everything else around them, forgetting that they both don't know anything at all about each other except their names, so far.

They felt something then, an indescribable feeling that they knew they shared.

When the boy turned to face them it was apparent why he was moving so awkwardly. His head was all smashed up, gashed open, blood flowing like a waterfall. His whole body was broken and disfigured, bones jutting out through flesh and skin, blood splattered all over his torn clothes. Patrick and Guy were both on the edge of their seats, gazing in awe and fright at what they were witnessing. The headlights of an approaching car illuminated the scars of that little boy and as it ran into him both Guy and Patrick blinked, their hearts jumping to their throats. When the car drove past, the boy vanished. There was no sign of him.

They both were looking at each other now, their eyes and mouths wide ajar. Each knew that the other has seen exactly the same thing, it was in their eyes but they struggled to accept it and fought hard to admit it. After a long moment of silence Patrick spoke, holding his drink.

"I'm not sure I want to drink anymore of that!"

"Do you know what just happened?" Guy said.

"I don't know. Maybe I don't wish to know, really. I honestly don't know," he replied, with conviction. After twisting and turning his thoughts, Patrick decided that Guy wasn't part of that drug gang, but instead was somehow going through the same things as he was going through. He didn't reveal these thoughts to him though.

"What made you come to me back at the funeral and ask to see me?"

Guy did not know how to answer that. He himself didn't know what pushed him to do it. He remembers feeling an urge to just walk up to him and tell him they should meet…for what he doesn't know.

"The only thing I can come up with is that something is trying to tell us something," said Guy.

"And what would that be? Of course you don't know, do you?"

Guy shook his head. The said: "Well, you ever get that feeling? Like you know someone? You think you've seen them before, somewhere, maybe in a dream? That might be it, you looked familiar."

"This is insane," said Patrick, now very disturbed and agitated, "I am fed up with this nonsense. I'm going home," And with that he strolled out of the bar.

"Enjoy your dreams, Patrick" whispered Guy, "and I'll enjoy mine,"

As both men walked their own almost-identical ways back to their homes, they hummed their favorite songs and pictured their fine memories. They looked at the sky above and counted the stars. They wanted to forget what had just happened and wanted to believe it was just a hallucination. That it meant nothing, that they are normal.

They flapped their arms up and placed their hands against the back of their heads and they each wished upon a falling star that they could get rid of all the madness in their lives. But they each knew, deep down inside, that it was no more than a wish.

Chapter 10

▼

It has been a little over a month since the funeral of Christina's mother, during which all four have not come across each other, save for Mandy and Patrick who met a few times. Their relationship was already starting to feel the strain. Their meetings, far and few between, had the atmosphere of a teenage couple out on a first date, nervy and clumsy, sometimes tense and electrified.

On one of these meetings Mandy inquired of her lover how he was doing in his job. The question upset him because it reminded him of the drug gang, which he hadn't told her about. He told nobody about it. They were sitting at a diner eating hamburgers and French fries just as the soft dark of autumn fell. The diner, which was owned by a short Jew with a bouncing belly, was packed, as it was Friday night. Lots of families, children yelling, loud and rowdy conversations. Patrick hated all that. It made him nervous. It didn't bother Mandy.

He'd been acting very suspiciously ever since that night, his eyes always darting about as if anticipating something that wasn't supposed to be there. When Mandy asked if something was wrong, he considered telling her, but then a crazy thought zapped through his mind like a bullet. What if she was with them? He asked himself mentally, and as soon as he completed the sentence in his mind he cursed and blamed himself for doubting his girlfriend. It was absurd! He felt disgusted at himself for even thinking it for a second. Why would he do that though? Why have it even crossed his mind? It was a thought that lasted for less than a second but one that now transformed Mandy's image in his mind and all these years of love and trust have started to fade away and dissipate like a cube of sugar.

It was a chilly early October afternoon, when Guy Kelton realized that soon he would have no money at all and that he will most probably be kicked out of the building. He has not paid the rent for more than three months. Soon he will be hungry and homeless. Thinking about finding a new job and working again makes him sicker than he already is.

Today, Guy decided he wanted to do something very different, something daring and challenging. Something that could change the way he has been spending his hours and days. Something dangerous, something exciting.

"Sick of this nark feeling I got in my guts. I want to do something that makes me smile and laugh at the people I hate," he said in a riling manner of speech to the doorman, Mr. Pickles—a fitting name indeed taking in mind his obsession for pickles.

"Well, da landlord iz pretty upset about you not payin' your dues Kel. You better do somethin' quick," warned Pickles, who was bemused that Guy stood by him at the gate of the building, actually chatting.

"He can go fuck himself in hell for all I care," Guy snapped.

He never saw the landlord during all the time he occupied the apartment on that third floor. He heard much about him though. He heard that the landlord, Conrad Spitfire, was a man of strict manner and low self-esteem and a man who would rather see his wife killed and daughter raped than lose his fortunes. He was one of the wealthiest and most powerful men in Okay but had always kept a low public profile. No one knew much about neither his personal life, nor his many businesses.

Both men stood, monitoring the people passing by them and observing the cars driving through Independent Avenue, where the building stood erect in line with other similar buildings. Some, of maybe five and eight floors, filled with apartments, others with two to three floors, were filled with small offices and shops.

As they stood, a black brand-new Chrysler Concorde with it's passenger non-other than Conrad Spitfire, drove by, with the chauffeur honking for pedestrians to clear the roads and stand back.

"Speak of da devil!' said the doorman, "Well, he's an ass-ole all right," He commented with a laugh.

A minute of silence followed and then the black man said "There was a brother livin' here with his young missus, few years back, just before you came in. Actually they were occupying your apartment, if I remember correctly," Mr. Pickles stopped and for a few short seconds seemed to try to conjure up his memories. He leaned his back on the wall and put his hands behind his back.

"They were a sweet couple. Very nice. The brother lost his job. Not sure why or how. He worked in some restaurant down town. Spitfire spat his fire on the poor fella just as soon as he heard the news. He didn't give him a chance to get another job; he didn't give him some time to collect his stuff. He just went up there with a couple of big guys and threw him and his pretty missus out. No one said anything. No one saw them 'round here again."

The men thought quietly for a while, Pickles thinking of the fate of the couple, of where the man and his wife are now, if they managed to survive. For a second, Guy thought he saw the old man's eyes water.

"But why?" he asked, trying to look as interested as he could.

"Maybe he kicked him out cuz he's black! And maybe nobody did nothin' cause we was all scared," said the mollified doorman.

Guy took his eyes away from the freckled face of Pickles and looked down at his feet. The story of the black couple sure did worry him. Would he end up like them? Being kicked out by two huge animal-men? As he looked at the ground, he saw an ant, a big black ant carrying a smaller one.

Guy bent down to get a closer look at them. The small ant looked hurt. He could see some of her legs missing. The big ant was helping the small ant. Guy found that very amusing. He stood up again. Looked at Pickles and then looked down again at the ants.

"How big is our world to them?" he said, nodding down towards the ants.

"Big enough to not need eyes to see it," replied Pickles, with a wide smile that showed his broken back teeth.

In the evening of that same day, Guy Kelton collected all the money he had, which was about forty dollars, sold everything precious and worthy he had, including his gold medal and cup which he won playing in the high school baseball team—the only reminders he took with him when he left his parents—and his mother's gold necklace which she gave him on his thirteenth birthday. He raised two hundred dollars and he went to Ashbed looking for a known criminal named GoGo.

Guy knew GoGo from school. When he was twelve, GoGo asked Guy to join his mob. Guy refused. But GoGo wouldn't let him go, he liked him, in his own fashion and he tried to tempt him, with money, candy, toys and stuff, but Guy didn't want to be part of it.

"I just want us to be pals, that is all," he told Guy.

Guy didn't find GoGo, but he found one of his boys, who guided him to another gangster, living in a dirty little room located on the roof of a building that housed a restaurant that Guy didn't recognize. This gangster would have what Guy requires. After some negotiations, Guy walked out of the gangsters' headquarters with a black Smith & Wesson 9mm pistol in his hand.

In another part of town, Christina Heywood was having sex with a man whose name she did not know, who she met in a bar that she has not been in before and she was as drunk as she has never been in her whole life. She was in her most vulnerable state, unaware of her actions, just wanting to escape her miseries and travesties.

Mandy and Patrick were sitting together on a comfy sofa watching television. Patrick was thinking of Christina, of her beautiful face and silky hair. He should not think of her but he does and worse than that, he feels he want to be with her so bad.

Mandy, meanwhile, sits on the sofa, beside him, placing her head over his chest, listening to his slow powerful heartbeats and fantasizing about another life in another place, thinking how beautiful their children would be.

Chapter 11

▼

"What is it?"

"Nothing,"

"Come on. You know you can tell me,"

"I am OK."

"No, you are not OK. You have not been OK since you started working again,"

He sighs and shakes his head. She grabs his hand and looks at him with sympathetic eyes.

"Please. Speak. Just let it out. Say it for love's sake."

He scratches his forehead. Sighs. Looks at her and says, "I think there's something wrong with my head!"

A sudden change of expression was visible on her face.

"What do you mean?" she asks.

"That's not all. My boss makes me run errands for his drug mob!"

Now the air in the room was filled with gloom. The couple were now sitting on separate chairs. A shiver ran through Patrick Roymint and there was a deep look on Mandy's face.

Earlier, before this conversation took place, Patrick committed the biggest mistake of his life. He confronted his boss, a thin, tall, bearded man, and informed him of his knowledge of the drug business he partakes in.

John Barton, the boss, is not a good man. He is a bad man, a very bad man. The deceptive kind. The kind that wears a perfect, nice mask to cover his ugliness. Barton is married to a lovely lady and has three children. He joined the company a long, long time ago. He was young then and began as a sales assistant.

He is now the head of marketing and sales. It's been twelve years for him here at Karmafoods.

It happened when Patrick came back from his latest errand, angry and malevolent, as he had dropped another drug package to that dreadful restaurant. He thought: I could stop this. I should stop this. But how?

Nevertheless he decided that something should be done before he got into trouble. Why did I have to go into that stupid place? Why did this happen? Why did I accept this job? All questions left unanswered.

After he told him, Barton threatened Patrick and ordered him to remain silent or he will lose everything he has, which wasn't much anyway. He also told him that he can't prove anything against him and that he, Patrick, is already considered a partner in the business.

His protests weren't of any use. He was helpless. Now, he is in a more messed up situation than ever. As he went over the whole situation with Mandy, she was, to his surprise, as calm as ever.

"So what will you do?" she asked him after a moment of silence.

"No idea. What will I do, Mandy?"

She leaned forward, sunk her head into her shaky hands and sighed deeply.

"I knew about all of it."

Patrick jumped at hearing this, shaking his head in disbelief. His mind was racing with thoughts, struggling to find the words to speak.

"I knew about it but I had to not say anything to anyone. I just wanted to make believe that I didn't know; didn't accidentally find a little plastic pack of white powder in Barton's office. I had to pretend it never happened."

She was now very distressed and her eyes were wet with glittering tears. There was no need to go on with the full story. Patrick got the whole picture. Mandy was caught in the same position as he was at the moment. But, he wondered, how could she have acted normally all this time? How could have she not said anything…to anybody…not even him? But what hurt him the most was that his earlier doubts were true.

"Have you seen Chrissy lately?" Patrick finally asked later that day, breaking the silence.

"What?"

"Christina," he corrected, "Have you seen her?"

There was a moment of stillness in the room before Mandy replied, "No. Haven't seen her for a few days now!" there was a short silence, as Mandy and

Patrick ate, broken only by dishes cluttering and mouths munching. Both knew the next question must be asked.

"Why ask?"

"I'm just trying to have a conversation here OK?" His voice was abnormally hard and stern. Mandy shrugged. More stillness.

She played with the peas on her plate with the fork. They were dining in her little apartment. She used to have a roommate. But she ran away with another woman, leaving Mandy paying the rent all on her own. As well as a big fat phone bill.

Patrick sighed, so did Mandy. They looked at each other. Mandy smiled first, he had to reply.

"Listen Pat, I think…' but she was interrupted by an unexpected knock on the door. Patrick looked at his girlfriend inquisitively, his eyes asking who that might be and Mandy's eyes saying she didn't have any idea.

The great shock she got when pulling the door open almost made her sick to the stomach.

It was Barton.

"Hello, my loyal and trusty subordinates," he sneered at them. Patrick stood up quickly and hurried to the door to block Barton's way.

"What do you want?" he said, looking at him with mad, hateful eyes.

"Uh, well, aren't you going to let me in first? I am your guest. Yes, indeed an unexpected one, but still,"

"An unwanted one," Stressed Patrick.

"And an unwelcome one too," came the low voice of Mandy, who stood helpless beside the door, looking at both men with bitter and solicitous eyes.

"We have to talk. I think you and I and—even our lovely Mandy here—know what about,"

"We have nothing to talk about. Now please leave us alone,"

"Afraid it's not that easy my friend,"

"I'm *not* your friend,"

"Oh yes. I am sorry. You aren't. Instead you are my errand boy," His eyes were gory; his smile was full of deception and indecency.

Both Patrick and Mandy knew that nothing good was going to come out of this.

Chapter 12

The day passed without anything worth mentioning, just hours, wasted, vanished, gone with the wind. The town is as good as dead. Going out doesn't seem to be helping much. There aren't many nice, quiet places to go to which would suit Guy's mood. And as for nightlife in Okay, it's too expensive and too silly to him. It was never his cup of tea. He hates clubbing; he finds them too noisy and stupid. People stacked in one small place like a pack of sweating dogs, dancing like crazy, drugging themselves with the ugly sounds of music, pounding beats that shake the earth and deafen the ears. It's another way to lose yourself and try to escape the harsh reality, a thing that Guy knows better not to fall into.

Right now, he's just driving his old battered car to wherever it takes him, and again, there aren't enough streets for him to wander around.

He was driving through Elmo Avenue, heading towards the busiest part in town, the one and only City Center. But of course it's only Tuesday and the streets and places aren't as busy as on weekends.

The car he hasn't been using at all lately. It was his father's; he just simply took off in it years ago when he left. The 35-year old Cadillac is so wrecked that it makes sharp, loud noises and bangs when you start it, when you brake, when you change the gear, when you turn, when you just about do everything and anything with it. It's a mess, but Guy never complained about it, except that it adds to his expenses. That's why he doesn't use it often. In fact it's been parked in the building parking lot for almost a year!

He looked out the car window on his left, a mid-aged man was walking on the side of the street, alone, head down, dragging his feet as slow as a turtle coming out onto the shore does. From that quick glance Guy knew how miserable and hopeless the man was. He looked lost in his own deep sea of scrambled thoughts.

Then a station wagon passed Guy; there was a cute little girl in the back of the car. She was happy, full of life, she looked at Guy and gave him a sweet little smile and waved at him, he smiled back. It took him some effort. It's hard for him to smile.

Now she, thought Guy, was blessed with ignorance, but once she grows up that smile will never surface again. Or at least, it won't be as honest and sincere as it is now.

He leaned forward to put the radio on and managed to place a tune from the local FM station. They were playing Britney Spears. They always do and God, how he hated that girl's voice. How could anyone listen to such synthetic voice? It's all fake. Everything was fake.

In the glove compartment, Guy found an old Nat King Cole tape. He put it on and the first song that played was 'Embraceable You'. It was a bit of surprise. He couldn't even remember listening to this record before. And he couldn't remember that his father was keen on music either. But it was so beautiful. It relaxed him and even made him smile.

Red light.

He almost didn't see it. He slowed down and stopped. Another car on the left side of the road also stopped and the man inside turned his head towards Guy Kelton and took a glance at him. He glanced back but made sure his eyes didn't meet with the man's, who looked unfriendly and as if he wanted vengeance. From whom? Guy thought. Probably life?

Ah, Green!

How weird people are in this town, he thought, after turning right towards the New City Coffee place, on Capital Avenue. Why is it that everybody seems angry at something, looking at strangers as if they were murderers? He parked the car on the side of the road, walked and went into the coffee place. It was a small place; one with red paint, a few tall chairs facing a large window, three tables were lined in one row, each with four chairs, all in black.

He ordered his usual regular house coffee with Irish crème, sat on his favorite chair just behind the window facing the street. Watching the lifelessness outside, while some jazz music, playing softly, came from the speakers above his head. The waiter came up to him with his drink.

"Here you go sir. Enjoy your coffee," he said with a smile.

Guy made a habit out of coming to this particular small coffee place down town. He likes drinking coffee. It makes him feel good. The aroma relaxes him.

Guy picks the cup of coffee and starts passing it under his nose, inhaling and exhaling slowly, but he does not take a sip, rather he replaces it back in front of him, taking a quick glance at the clock on the wall, it's something to eight.

Guy sighed and began to observe the movements of objects around him, in front of him. He sees a car, another one, and another, where are these people going? What are they rushing for? He then noticed an old woman walking down the pavement, attempting to cross the road, she might as well die now, he reckoned of her. He looked down at the cup.

He started thinking about all the weird things that have happened to him. The strange alley with the tall wall, the old man, the huge black gate, his meeting with Patrick, the wicked dream with the king and his brother, Morris. Oh it's been such a long time since he last saw him.

Morris left the town when he was twenty, straight after completing his two-year diploma course at the Borough Local College. He left all the shit behind him in Okay and went on in search of a new, better life out there. It's been eight years. No visits, no calls, no letters. Nothing.

Guy again looked out the window. Down on the far left corner, a young boy, a beggar, with a torn shirt and shredded pants, was sitting on the pavement. What future has this boy? Guy wondered. Absolutely nothing but suffering and pain. He will forever beg for shelter and food, until he dies. Again, he might as well just die now!!

Finally, he takes his cup again, and sips some of the drink. He, Guy, might as well die now too. Drink the coffee, just drink…don't think, he tells himself, but of course he can't *not* think, no matter how hard he tries to shut his mind off. One cannot just ignore all the things that have so twisted and crippled your life. These things ought to be thought of, whether one desired it or not.

Guy found this revelation to be very fascinating. He was more amused however, when he further thought of it and realized that the mind never stops thinking. It keeps going on and on and on. And we keep talking to ourselves, within ourselves. Not for a fraction of a second do we stop talking or thinking. Even when we sleep, the minds live their own life through dreams. The mind does what it desires and lives how it wants. The powers of the mind in producing these emotionally scary dreams, never failed to amaze Guy. How it could convince us that these dreams become our reality.

Guy Kelton has been dreaming of traveling the world, of dancing in a beautiful city, of things he wants to see and things he wants to do. But these dreams have always scared him, even though they sound wonderful, they are scary because of what could happen and it's not like dying, having an accident or being killed by someone or something.

He gets a worrying feeling about these dreams. Something deep inside him tells him it is not right, that it bears a bad thing. Something tells him these dreams should be forgotten.

Forever.

A sudden loud scratching voice awakened Guy from his meditation and brought him back to reality. There was a sound of rubber burning on an asphalt road, followed by a big blow, and broken glass. Guy jumped and looked out through the window across the street.

A little body, covered in blood, twisted in a most gruesome position, was lying on the middle of the street. The young boy, the beggar, has just been hit by a monstrous pick-up truck. He was dead.

People ran out of the shop, passers-by stood in silence and so did the male driver. No one tried to approach the body. No one wanted to get closer and see the splattered blood and flesh. Suddenly it seemed all so very familiar. Guy picked himself up and walked out the place and headed for his car, not looking behind. Not even once.

Chapter 13

▼

Young blossoming tulips stand tall and glorified on one of the many display shelves as the old man arranges a bouquet for a gentleman who seemed to be running out of patience.

The shop, a little narrow place with oak-wood interior, was intoxicated with the smell of luscious perfumes.

"Hurry up please," he urged.

But the old man, sitting tranquilly on an old wooden chair, wasn't paying much attention to him, or to his inpatient attitude. All of his attention was directed unconditionally to the bunch of flowers, jasmines and roses he's making the bouquet with.

"Come on old man I need that today!"

The flower man, now busy with the final touches of the remarkably beautiful bouquet he's prepared, looked up at the man, who is not any more gentle now as when he first arrived, and said in a calm voice.

"You see, that's why I love flowers, they don't get angry. They don't talk like us. They don't talk at all!"

"Oh great now he's bullshitting," the customer was more talking to himself now than to the old man. The latter chuckled at the rudeness of his customer, he is used to such treatment.

"Do you want flowers that can say all that you want to say without having to utter a word, or do you want a crippled bunch of dying colored papers in a plastic sack?"

The man was more than pleased with the final result. That was pretty much apparent in his face as he held it in his hands. The bouquet was perfect; it was filled with colours, of flowers and roses of all kinds, so shimmering and radiant.

The gentleman looked at them and was fascinated. He smelled them and he felt an urge to smile and laugh. And he did.

"Look I'm sorry Sir. It's just that I'm in a hurry. I don't want to miss it, she'll get mad and all,"

"It's all right, I know," the old flower man said, as he ran his right hand to the back of his head to brush the grey strands of his receding hair.

"It's okay. You don't have to be sorry,"

The gentleman reached into his jacket pocket and passed money to the old man. He took it and proceeded to get the change for his customer.

"It's all righty. You earned it," said the gentleman in the brown suit, "Thanks,"

"Well, you're welcome," replied the old man, "May God bless you, son," Then he turned to his colored children to take care of them.

When Christina Heywood woke up, she announced to herself, sorely and with fatigue, that she was having a dream hangover. A dream hangover, that's when you wake and feel like a ten ton hammer was hammered on your head, when you feel the sides of your head so stoned, your thoughts blocked, your eyes burning, and you can only try and find out what were you dreaming. Flashes struggle to surface, recollecting only bits and pieces that don't make any sense.

"Stupid-God-damned-fucked-up dreams," she angrily muttered as she rubbed the back of her hands against her waking, pretty eyes.

She turned to look at her wristwatch on the bedside table. It wasn't there. She didn't want to get up and look for it though, not now, not this very moment. She threw back her head on the pillow and just then she realized that she was naked!

It surprised her to be naked under the sheets, she has never slept naked before, she never even considered it. What made her do it she didn't know, and right this very minute, she didn't care. If it had happened before all of this, before she lost her lover, before she was fired from her job, before her mother died, before making love to a nobody, she would have cared.

She stood unwillingly and marched towards the mirror in the bathroom wondering what she was becoming. She washed her face of the sorrow and paleness that painted it and looked at her own beautiful naked body. And for once, she felt exposed within herself.

Christina put on her robe and walked down to the kitchen. She was just about to call to her mother when she remembered that she no longer existed in life. Her name was dangling on the tip of her tongue.

Natalie.

She made herself a quick, very strong cup of coffee and started drinking it, without cream or sugar, which was unusual for her. She likes her coffee very white and sweet. She thought she ought to try it this way, might help her shake off the dizziness of her dream hangover.

The fridge offered nothing to Christina to kill her hunger. Not having anything to eat added up to her late morning wake-up misery. Out of the blue, and from the deep hidden memories in the back of her head, Aaron Minster jumped into Christina's fuzzy thoughts.

She thought of their good times. Their best moments together, when he would show up early in the morning, before Christina would go to work, to take her to their favorite spot, and have a nice, quiet morning breakfast picnic at the riverside, in a place called Waterbed—she always wondered why most places have the word BED at the end—about forty minutes from the city center, which is a very long and unworthy ride for most of the town folk to bother make for their luxury.

There they would sit alone, on the yellow grass, watching the few early birds humming and singing and flying across the clear flowing river, its water running through the finely-shaped cobblestones. They would have pancakes with strawberry and raspberry jam and honey and milk and everything that is sweet and nice. They would hold each other, kiss, and lay, staring up at the sky for a few minutes before getting off to work.

How sweet were those mornings. How calm and tender was the ambience. How romantic and gentle was Aaron. Where would he be right now? She found herself wondering. Would he be doing the same with his new lover? Or would he wake up one morning and find himself wondering about Christina and their times together just like she is?

"Don't do it Chrissie," she whispered to herself "Don't even think about it."

In fifteen minutes, Christina was on her way to Aaron Minster's work place. She wore something simple, something Aaron always liked to see her in: A pair of dark blue jeans and tight v-neck, white T-shirt. She put on sunshades and her white trainers.

It was around nine o'clock. The most beautiful time of day for Christina, though it's been such along time since she last enjoyed it.

"What's so special about this time of day?" Mandy asked her once. Christina told her it was the only time in life that she would feel alive, the only time that loves just being free of obligations, doing what she always liked to do without rushing herself and saying there isn't enough time. It is when she wakes and goes out at such time that she would truly feel she lived the day to the fullest and made the best out of it.

Today, she hopes she would feel alive again. Even if for just this one more time only.

Aaron works at a computer software firm in the biggest and tallest building in Okay. It's a twelve-story building and any person from town has not seen anything taller and bigger than this building. The Doyen Tower. That's what it's called.

More than twenty years ago one of the huge investment firms wanted to put some money into town. They thought they could come up here and modernize the town and drive it into the new millennium by establishing a complex to house the biggest and best computer and technology companies. Of course they were wrong, they made a costly mistake. They didn't do their full research apparently. They didn't put into their minds that the people of Okay are not very keen on such ideas, matter of fact they are not keen on any sort of idea. They never liked technology much. The company wasted their money, done the project in a record breaking time, but wasted their money. Only one computer firm got into the business. The one Aaron's working for. Half of the building has always been empty. There are even some parts that have not ever been used. That investment firm was bankrupt after three years and the town municipality now runs the building.

To save time, Christina took a cab. Cabs are rare to find here, simply because people don't need them. Most places are just a walking distance in town, besides almost everybody has a car here. For a small compact town, Okay is considered one of the most congested areas around.

There aren't a lot cabs though, Christina reckons she counted fifteen only. She knows because each cab driver has a different name for his blue cab. She can't remember the last time she took one.

She rode with Mark Hudson who calls his cab Bluesea. Hudson is a single man in his mid forties. He was married to a Persian lady once. They were both cheating on each other so when they each found out they confronted and left each other peacefully.

Anyway, Christina got in the back. They greeted each other. She told him to take her to the Doyen Tower. He asked her if she's going there to meet her boyfriend. She frowned and remained silent. He said he could remember he once took here there before, almost six months ago. Still she did not say a word. He apologized and said it was probably none of his business. She nodded and silently faded into a web of thoughts.

An image of her dead mother appeared in front of her eyes. A picture of her long-gone dad in her younger days manifested itself as a hologram walking the streets of Okay. For a mere second, she almost believed it was real. Where would he be now? Is he doing fine? Is he married? Does he have children? Is he alive?

Looking through the window, Christina saw life in Okay as she hasn't seen before. She saw people walking dragging their feet into oblivion. She saw stores and shops empty but of their owners and staff. She saw strangers driving their cars to destinations known only to them. She saw unhappy children. She saw so many things and in the end she saw her reflection on the window and she knew that she was just another person. She saw Okay for what it really is. Just a ghost town. Filled with lost and tortured souls. There was no place for dreams here. This was a dreamless town.

They reached the block where she used to work. She looked to her right and saw the building that housed the Karmafoods company. It was an awful place to work in Christina realized now. She was glad she was not there anymore. She thought of Mandy, probably getting herself busy typing some worthless reports right at that minute.

As she looked to her left, she saw the flower store. She quickly ordered Hudson to stop and drop her there.

"OK Miss! Hope things are alright with you?" he said. He was a good man. Seemed very kind and gentle.

"I'm fine, thanks," she said, climbing out of the cab, "Here, keep the change,"

"Thank you, Miss. Have a nice day,"

There was a man inside the shop. Hmm, that's not usual. Not so many people are keen on flowers anymore, except maybe for special occasions. Christina could hear the man nagging about something. She stood near the door in a position that no one would notice her.

After a few moments, the man emerged from inside and Christina, as soon as she felt him moving out, pretended that she had just arrived and was about to go in. As they passed each other, they did not look at each other.

The man was looking at the flowers, and Christina was looking down and arranging her hair in a most peculiar and wonderful way. A way that was so familiar to the passing man that he couldn't help but look behind himself and take a glance at that beautiful woman.

For a long second he stood still, as if the whole world froze around him.

"Christina" he said but it was too low. "Christina!" he called again, louder this time. This time Christina heard him well and turned towards him, just to receive a great shock. The man standing there, with the beautiful bouquet of flowers in his hand, was none other than Aaron Minister.

They came closer to each other, taking slow and careful small steps. All of a sudden both their hearts jumped out of their chests. Their hearts were their guides now. Not their minds. They stayed silent, both knowing that any word spoken might ruin the whole scene. The whole beauty of this remarkable moment. They hugged, a powerful and passionate hug, their arms wrapped around each other, their hearts beating against each other, breathing down each other's necks.

It felt like they were finally back home.

Chapter 14

Holding the gun in his hand felt strange. It scared him, yet gave him some sort of confidence and strength that he had never experienced before. He ran his fingers over its smooth, cold, edgy features and then put it into the glove compartment of his father's old car.

As he opened it, a little photo fell down. He picked it up and looked at it. It was of his father; looking young and happy and youthful in that frozen moment. Guy could barely recognize him. His face was brighter and rounder, his greasy thick hair swept to the side. He was smiling. Guy couldn't tell how old that photo was but what struck him the most was that in that photo, standing right next to his father, dressed smartly, smoking a cigar, was a man who his father always hated and detested and never spoke a good word of. Yet there he was, standing next to him, arm over his shoulder, smiling.

The man in the photo was the Mayor of Okay. For a moment Guy wasn't sure it *was* him; he looked very different from how he looks now. In the photo he is quite slim and as young, if not younger, than his father.

Mayor Leon Cunningham, who's been in office ever since Guy can remember, is a person who loves to be glorified, loves to be in control of things. And he was Guy's father's best friend. The two promising young politicians were very close. They had plans and hopes for this town and they wanted to achieve them together. But then, somewhere down the years, something went terribly wrong between them. And the two close friends and political partners became sworn enemies. But of course Guy didn't know any of that. His father kept it all a secret from him, from everyone around him. All Guy knew was that his father had hatred and dislike for that man. He would turn the television off whenever the

Mayor came on and would skip any page with his picture in the newspaper. Which confused Guy as to why his father had that picture here? He also wondered how he could not have seen it before as it sat there in the car all these years. He had always wanted to build up the courage to ask his father about it all but never did.

Perhaps he can now. He suddenly decided to pay his old man a visit. He slipped the photo in his shirt pocket and drove off.

Carter Jay Kelton, now in his late sixties, still lives with his wife, his school-sweetheart, in the same dusty house as he has for the past thirty years in the oldest area of the town, Blossomville, the area that used to be the heart of the town, where all people happy and shiny lived. It was the district that people came to for a simple walk among its green streets and cozy wooden cottages. It was the glittery and fancy part of Okay with pretty big houses and wonderful, lovely streets.

Now it is no more than domicile for ghosts. A ghastly place where you can find empty, crinkled houses and lonesome, pathetic streets, where one would not feel any warmth in its coldness. All the beauty has turned into ripe ugliness, like the face of a beautiful woman in her dying years. This district once blossomed. And everything and everyone with it did. But then it stopped blossoming. It had to, for everything has to come to an end, and everything sweet and pretty, ends quicker and sooner than any other thing.

Guy had grown up seeing the area turn from gold to dust, being transformed over the years into a dead, petal-less flower and seeing it again now depressed him gravely, adding to his life's sad miseries.

As he drove through the filthy streets, he was startled by a smashing sound, followed with loud laughter. Guy looked to his left to see a black young boy running away with a big smile on his face, being chased by a fat man, stark naked save for tight shorts, waving a baseball bat.

Guy didn't know whether to worry about what that boy had done or smile at the sight of the fat man behind him.

A moment and a turn later, he approached his childhood home. It was sitting there in the middle, flanked by two similar houses on each side.

Guy parked the car in front of his house. Well, these houses, they used to call them villas, they are more like ancient shanties now. Villa Number 1810, Rosegarden Road, Blossomville. That's where Guy lived with his wayward family for his first twenty years or so.

The mesmerized young man stood at the thin, falling picket fence for a moment, before pulling the courage to walk in. A long, pitiful walk it seemed.

Guy, while strutting his way to the door, looked at the yard, once to his left and once to his right, and was taken back to the years when he was a little boy playing with his brother. The colorful swing-boat, which Guy spent most of his outside time on, now sits like the broken, sunken Titanic on the ground, its colors all faded. The front-yard seemed like a battlefield where one or two rusty toys still lay abandoned; its grass all dead and dry from the sweltering sun and the once-magical orchestra of orchids—his mother's favorite—flattened to the ground.

Finally, he reached the door. He was hesitant; should he knock or should he just walk in like nothing happened, pretend as if he had not walked away from them, as if he had not disappeared without a word for four years? This, he decided, won't be very pleasant.

"Why am I here?" he asked himself "What am I doing?" He tried to understand his urge to come over after all these years, was it the photo? Was it fear? Was it loneliness? Maybe regret?

Knock, knock! No answer. Another few knocks and still no reply. Perhaps they are out? He turned and started to walk away. A thought: Perhaps they have died. But there was a light inside, maybe it was a stranger, maybe the house has been rented out, maybe he, Guy, is thinking too many thoughts that were ambiguous and lame.

He turned back again and just as he was about to give it another go, the door opened, just.

"What do you want?" a snappy voice Guy didn't recognize blurted from behind the door.

"It's me!" he replied. How stupid that sounded. It's me? That's not an answer. Why do people say that? "It's Guy," he corrected, "Is that you dad?" a few seconds of silence.

"What do you want?"

"It's your son," sighed Guy, "Don't you remember me?"

The old man standing at the door, who looked more bald and short and bellied than Guy remembers, stared at Guy for a mollified moment with blood-shot, little eyes, that seem almost closed. Then, he shrugged. Guy prudently gave up. It was hopeless he thought.

"It's OK. I'll go, sorry," he said, and then whispered, "It was a mistake."

The gruntled old man stepped out and away from the door. "Of course I remember you, you stupid, back-stabbing piece of pig-shit!"

Guy, surprised and taken by the outburst, turned back again and looked in astonishment as his father, now standing at the door with both hands in his trouser pockets.

"You didn't answer me boy. What the hell do you want?"

A moment of silence this time prompted a challenging eye contact between estranged father and son. Guy ended it by opening up his arms, shrugging: "I just wanted to talk to you, that's all. I…I," He wanted to say miss you but couldn't. But the truth of it was that he himself didn't know "I wanted to see you and talk,"

Jay stared at his son pensively, grunted and then stepped aside, making way for Guy to walk in.

Nothing much had changed inside the house. The same furniture, the same trivial ornaments, but the serene calmness of it is now long gone, no traces of it could be found. It had an awful stench of smoke and alcohol. It was dark.

The old man was already seated as Guy kept looking around the house. "Where's the television set?"

"Burned it,"

"Burned it!" A short pause to think of a better word didn't work. "Why?"

"Well,"

Guy waited. It seemed that the question made his father more uncomfortable.

"'Cause bastards keep showing these fucking dirty movies all the time. Fagots keep fucking each other over and over again," he said, rubbing his wrinkled forehead, "So I burned the damned thing."

Guy could have asked a thousands questions. But he didn't. He simply dismissed it. "Fair enough," was all he said. He looked for a place to sit. The green sofa.

"Don't set there." snapped Jay at his son. Guy froze his seating process mid-air. His father nodded to him to sit on the wooden chair beside the square coffee table. Guy didn't know what was going on, this wasn't how he remembered his father. This was just a crazy, old bitter man.

Both men sat silently, waiting for each other to say something. It was Guy who did. "So, how's mom? Where is she by the way? I'd like to see her."

"She's in her bedroom," answered Jay, "What did you want to talk about?" he added as he drew a cigar out of the left pocket of his thin, maroon cardigan.

"Dad, that's a cigar!" said Guy as his old man looked for a lighter.

"Yes. Yes it is." he answered.

"You never smoked, dad."

"Well I do now, so piss off."

Guy scratched his scalp trying to find a reason behind this change in his father, who was still looking for his lighter. His head rolled and turned until it stopped straight at the desk light on the coffee table Guy was sitting beside. The lighter was there. He played with his eyes, looking at Guy and then at the lighter almost simultaneously. Guy caught the drift. He picked it up and stretched himself to light the cigar for his father and sat back again.

His father started puffing the cigar with utmost pleasure. Guy held the lighter for a while in his had and gazed at it. It was made of what he reckoned it to be silver and ivory.

"Nice. Must have cost you, this lighter?"

"Yeah,"

The rattled son replaced his father's expensive lighter and took a deep breath. He didn't expect it to be such an overwhelming experience. This was his home, this was his father and somewhere here was his mother. But what did he miss? His father was always indifferent to him and kept a distance, but he's never been as bitter. He had to know. Something had happened and he wouldn't know without asking.

"What happened dad?"

"God fucked us, that's what happened," came another snappy reply. Jay took another lengthy puff. The ash fell down onto him.

"Dad, this is not you. You are not like that. You are a good person, why would…" Jay interrupted this furiously "What do you know you little dick? You walked out on us, leaving us high and fucking dry and then after all these years you come in here "to talk" with your crazy old man! Don't you try pretending to be the good person here. Don't come back preaching, pretending like you care."

Of course, his brother left them as well but Guy knew it was for the better to not mention him now. He was not here. He was far away. He was forgotten.

"I know what you are thinking now. You're thinking 'Well Morris walked out on you too'. Just for your information, he has been helping us out all these years, sending us money, things. Even calling from time to time," A short stop to gasp some air, and a puff of course, "And if you must know, he is coming over in a couple of weeks. He is getting married."

Too much information, too many things Guy was unaware of. All this was happening without him knowing. But it was his own fault and just now, he was beginning to regret it.

"I'm…Well, I'm sorry dad. For all it's worth,"

"Too late for sorries," Jay whispered as he coughed several times, before deciding it was better for him to put out the cigar. The smoke hung in the air right above the old man's head for a long moment before slowly climbing higher and vanishing. Guy was getting uncomfortable in his seating, he was thinking of standing up and walking around the room, but that would irritate his father more.

Jay leaned forward, sitting his elbows on his thighs. "You know, son. I am an old man, maybe not that old, but I am old. I don't have a job, I don't have money, I don't have good health, I don't have friends, they've all moved away, I don't have a family and I don't have a…" His eyes were getting watery. He sniffed. "That's what life does to you and the worst part is you have to accept it and live with it," He wiped his eyes with the back of his left hand and sat back again.

"You remember dad? How I was so crazy about baseball? You weren't much of a fan but when I watched a game, you would sit beside me and we'd watch the game together. You'd always pick the team playing against my team and you'd get so involved, just to see my team was beaten. We'd make fun of each other every time our team won." Guy's eyes were now beginning to sting as well. "Dad, you taught me good things. A lot of good things. And as any other father you had your faults, but I loved you and I guess I always will, inside. And I guess I have always had a problem in expressing myself. Always had a problem in…Well, you know."

"I guess I do." They both looked down, hoping for this awkward, warm moment to pass quickly "Would you want to see your room?"

The room, is it still there? Guy didn't know why he was so surprised by that.

"Yes, sure. I would love to."

The walk up the stairs and down through the hall was retrograding. Guy, during the short trip to his room, relived most of his happy moments. Images flashing in his head of his younger self, as a kid, as a teenager. Images he had forgotten, neglected and ignored, locked deep inside his mind along with all the old memories he had.

His room was the last one along the hall to the right, facing his brother's room, which was much bigger than his. It didn't bother him though that he had the smaller room, as long as he could do anything he wanted in it. As his father opened the door and let himself in, Guy had a nervous outburst of emotions. It was in this little moment that he was captured in limbo.

It was there, all of it. Untouched. Untampered with. The huge baseball players' posters, pictures of his favorite singers and actresses, the records, the books, the bed that he would have liked to be bigger, the desk and most importantly his own personal ball corner. He took a couple of steps and stood in the center of the room, looking around at all the things that he left behind. The things that used to form his life. A different life, a life he doesn't recognize anymore. In that special corner of his, he arranged all the things related to his beloved game in a soulful way. There was a picture with him with his favorite pitcher, a ball he collected at a league game. His own record book, little souvenirs and ornaments and a small diary.

He picked that up, his father tentively watching him, a calm smile on his face. He opened it and read it. It was the book he kept all his figures of every ball game he has played since the age of ten: Strikes, balls, fouls, hits, home runs. The whole deal.

At the age of six, Guy wanted to be a pilot, or at least that's what he thought. He used to dream of flying across the world in his own tiny jet. Travel over the farthest seas and to the most foreign of lands. That was the dream he shared with everyone.

"So kiddo, what do you want to be when you grow up?" someone would ask. "A pilot!" he'd gaily say. And they would laugh at his face. The kind of laugh that they'd think a kid would think is to comfort and encourage him. But in truth it was one that made a kid feel ridiculed and hopeless. Disappointed in his dream and in himself.

The true dream he lived though was of being a professional baseball player. He was good and he had talent. Everybody knew that, but they ignored it, even his parents. At school he was the best player. He pitched and he hit like no other kid around. He continued playing up to his high school years, until he dropped out of the school team because he thought that was what his parents wanted. He thought it would be better for him and his studying. But he was wrong and he knew it.

That dream he kept for himself. Never shared it with any soul. He kept it within him, until it faded and died away. Now when he looks back, he regrets letting go of his dream. He should have never given up on it. He should have fought for it and he should have not let anyone tell him otherwise.

One day, when he was little, he came from a game so happy and joyful. He led his team to yet another glorious win. He came home determined to tell his dad about how good a player he is, how talented and skillful in the game, how he wanted to be a professional ball player. How that was his biggest dream.

"Dad," he said, "I'm so good at this. I think I could be a great player." he wanted to say more but waited to first see his father's reaction.

"Do whatever you want to do," he told him. Then added "just don't screw up at school." But he had said it in a manner that made Guy feel very bad; the indifference in his father's tone took away all his determination and joy. When he said the same thing to his mother on another occasion, she told him the same, but in a more friendly and caring manner, with a warm, gentle smile on her face.

He hasn't played baseball for more than six years now. All that he can do now is just sit on his butt, drink a beer and watch the real pros play in the major league. The enjoyment of watching it only brings a bit of bitterness at the end as it conjures up all these memories and possibilities of the life and dream he could have had.

A ball, a bat, a glove and a cap all sat silently near the corner. He bought those with all the money he collected through a whole year. He'd had to get them through mail order, as none of the local stores stocked decent baseball gear then.

He put on the cap and grabbed the bat first and gave it a light slow swing, squeezing the handling-end hard. Then he put on the glove and held the ball in his right hand. It felt great. It felt as if he were holding the whole world in his hand for a mere second.

"Thank you, dad." He said. But his father was already gone.

Chapter 15

There was sudden silence looming in the house Guy noticed as he left his room. The thought of calling his father's name crossed his mind, but the calmness and quietness of the house compelled him to remain silent. It was the sort of atmosphere you get in a low-budget horror flick, where one of the fill-in characters roams aimlessly around the house of fright to have his head chopped off by a skeleton with an axe just around a corner.

The walls were blackened and the corridor was darkened, by something. The wooden floor no longer creaked under his footsteps. The corridor seemed longer than Guy remembers. Now it seemed to stretch forever. Guy's steps were getting slower and heavier. His whole body was heavy. He decided to shout out to his father, but he couldn't, as if some crow had snatched his tongue and flown afar with it.

The house looked more and more unfamiliar to him with every slow, heavy step he took. He finally reached his parents' room—or at least what looked like his parents room—approached the door and began opening it. Again, he sensed something abnormal and out of place lurking within the walls and air of the house.

He began to feel exhausted. Sweat pouring from his forehead. He gasped for air with difficulty. His body felt heavier than his feet could carry. As he went in, he was reassured that it was his parents' room. He wondered why he doubted it in the first place. The room was dark as well. All he could see were unclear lines and shapes. The only light in the room was near the bed, which from the look of it seemed to be occupied by someone.

Must be mother, reckoned Guy. With half a step, he was already by the bed. The change of speed shocked him and he was almost certain that what was happening was unreal, but for that moment it was and it did not seem pleasant. It was happening again, he knew it.

"Mom?" he whispered, and came no reply. Then again louder "Mother?"

The person on the bed did not say anything, move or even breathe. It was still. Guy fell down on his knees, by the bed. When he looked straight ahead to the window, he saw an owl. It was a white owl. It sat at the edge of the window. Its eyes were golden and sharp. In the background, Guy saw black clouds forming, and a curved, very thin line that might have been the moon. The whole place was deadly silent. Is she dead? He wondered, feeling frail and exposed. He felt a sudden chill.

In one sudden move, Guy felt his right hand reaching for the person on the bed. As he touched the figure a heinous scream pierced his ears. The voice was so rendering and raucous, like a chainsaw cutting through a wall of bricks. Guy's mind went blank for a short moment. He did not know anything at all. Not knowing where he was, who he was and what was happening. In that moment he could not think of as simple a thing as a bird or a chair or even a pen.

He tried to picture something, anything, but failed. His mind was empty for that moment and even though it was very short, it inflicted a fear that he has not ever felt and probably would never feel again. The thoughts of his mind were so fast, travelling through the cells of his brain ten times the speed of light and he felt his head was close to exploding. But these thoughts were just a blur, they never settled for him to properly acknowledge them. It was a moment of utter ignorance.

Then he heard a voice calling his name and at the same speed of those thoughts he remembered all the things that he was trying to remember. The place was suddenly aglow, radiating with light. Someone had switched on the lights and Guy felt a terrible pain in his eyes. The same pain he feels every time he wakes up from a long sleep in a lighted room.

"Son! What are you doing?" It was his mother. She startled him. He turned to steal a glance and then turned back again at the bed. It was empty. It took a while for him to adjust his eyes to the new light. He shook off the strange dizziness and massaged his face with both his hands. He kept staring at the bed.

"What's wrong son?"

Finally he said "Nothing mother. I was just looking for you,"

She opened her arms to hug her son just like a bird would fold its wings over it's yet to hatch eggs. He gladly responded to her.

"Good to see you mother."

No response. But he could feel the beats of her broken heart as she began to quietly weep. Guy backed up a little and looked at his mother's face. It was the same face, the same features, and the same lines. Just like he remembers her, unlike his father.

"I am sorry mom," he sorrowfully said, each word filled with deep sadness and regret.

His mother looked up at him, drew her hand back and smacked him on the face, a gentle slap on his right cheek, a slap of a mother who had dearly missed her son.

"Bad boy! You are a bad boy," she said, stressing each word and biting her teeth together. She was angry. She was frustrated. Just like any mother would feel if she had been neglected by her son for four years, dumped, after all those years of loving and caring and raising.

They both sat on the bed, Guy holding his mother's hand and she holding a handkerchief she'd pulled from her dress pocket in the other. The dress was white and long and baggy and had little patterns of flowers and other nice things.

Guy didn't know what to say. Nothing he could say now that could ease the pain of all those empty, sad years that his mother, and probably his father too, had gone through. He tried to think of something. Tried to think of a reason why he never came back earlier? What happened that made him so emotionless, so selfish? Perhaps it was one of the things that people do without a reason, he thought, maybe someone up there sometimes decides to make one do what one is not supposed to do. Sometimes a person would just do something that hasn't been in his mind at all. It just pops up and you do it without second thoughts. Strange thought. But the true answers were there within him, somewhere in his mind, he just instinctively blocked them away.

That year, the year he left, Guy had received all the punches a teenager could ever get. He was cheated on and dumped by his girlfriend, the one who he truly and madly loved. He got a final warning by the school because he wasn't doing well and he would be kicked out. It made him rethink his decision to stop chasing his dream because that was all he could think about, all the time, especially during class. But even that was shattered when he broke his wrist.

He had been unwillingly helping his father move a cupboard and his hand was stuck between the piece of heavy wooden furniture and the wall. It was the most painful thing he'd ever been through. His wrist was damaged badly and the doctors told him that his wrist movement and hand control would never be the same again and that the chances of him ever going pro were nil. He was very angry with his father up to the point of accusing him that he did it on purpose. It was that incident that really triggered his need to walk away.

"I was foolish. I know that now. But I hope you understand. I beg for your forgiveness." He said.

His mother could sense that he was holding back his tears. So was she, but she did not say anything. She played with her handkerchief and looked away.

"I just can't explain what happened. I can't come up with any excuses." He added.

His mother was still hesitant to speak. She drew her hand from his grip. Guy looked down and then stared at the palms of his hands as if he were reading his fortune. He couldn't find anything cheerful. They were plain and empty, reflecting only sadness and pain.

Supporting himself on his knees, he stood up and said: "No words I know can describe my sorrow and regret and nothing I could say could make things any better. Just wanted to try, I guess." He made for the door.

"Did you see your father?" asked Mary-Moon, as Guy reached the door. That was her name. Mary-Moon. Her father had named her after Marilyn Monroe because it had been *his* father's wish before he died to have a granddaughter named after the famous dead actress. But as she grew older, people began calling her Mary-Moon.

"Yes." Replied Guy, without turning to her.

There was a long silence. Guy could feel his heartbeats and hear his own heavy breathing. And his mother's.

"After you left us," she began "everything we ever dreamed of, everything we worked for, was destroyed. We failed. It was too much to take,"

Guy turned to her. Stood at the door. His face had an anxious look on it. He wanted to hear this.

"We were trying to get you a scholarship in college in another place. Some place big. Even your brother was trying to help us get it. It was going to be a surprise. But then you had that accident and you left. You just don't have any idea how awful it made your father feel, to be the one who hurts you the most. Sure, he didn't want his son to be just a ball player in this lousy place. He…we wanted to give you a better life, away, a place with opportunity, where you could stand on your own feet.

"It did take a while, but finally he understood how much it meant to you. How much you loved to play. But I guess it was a little bit too late. Even I was too late."

Guy again approached his mother; he sat on his knees in front of her, and looked at her through the eyes of a child who is being told a tale, a sad tale. She rubbed her old hands on his cheeks and he felt the roughness of the skin of her hands.

It all made sense to Guy now. He was the source of all this misery for his parents. He destroyed his father. He destroyed this house, which used to be so lovely and warm and tender. He dropped his head on his mothers lap and began to cry, "I don't know what is wrong with me. Why am I like this? Why is God punishing me?"

"Shush, my boy. It's all right. Sometimes God tests people by making them go through such things. You just have to keep your faith. Have faith in whatever it is that you believe is right. Have faith in yourself and believe in yourself. You will be alright, darling."

For a brief moment they both fell silent. Not speaking a word. Just shedding tears over the wasted years. About the things that have made their lives too twisted and gypped to celebrate.

"I'd better go now." Said Guy, before standing up, kissing his mother's forehead and heading towards the door again. "I will come back again I promise."

"Soon?"

"Very soon." he whispered.

There was gap between the last sentence and the next. As if both did not want this to end. As if they had more things to be said and more questions to be asked. But something dark and old prevented them

"It was nice seeing you again son." They both smiled and shyly waved good-bye.

Guy wanted to say good-bye to his father too, but he couldn't find him anywhere in the house. He also couldn't fight the desire to go back to his room and pick up his favourite baseball.

Chapter 16

▼

A few old fat men sat at the bar with beers in their hands. Cracking sad and pathetic jokes about lousy sex and skinny mannequins and telling each other to forget about the past, about their long-gone youth, and to dance for the moment.

The bar used to be a little diner many years ago, the most famous in the district. Ironically, the owner died of food poisoning he got from something he ate from his own diner. His son, a beer-fanatic, liked the idea of having free beer for himself. So, he turned the inherited diner into a bar serving nothing but cheap local beer.

His name is Barry. His regular customers called him Beery. He loves beer so much that he even tried to change his name to Beer Cohol—the second name obviously from the word alcohol. The court didn't give him what he wanted though. They told him beer manufacturers wouldn't allow it, which was just about as bullshit as anything else the Okay court says.

A broken jukebox of old honky-tonk songs stood silently against the wall. Cigarette butts scattered over the floor. A neon sign saying BEER IS HEAVEN dangling on the ceiling flickered. The place was utter filth. It smelled of sweat and cigarette smoke and booze.

On a lone chair in the farthest corner of the bar sat Carter Jay Kelton.

He comes to the bar almost every night and stays almost until closing time. Jay, for a reason he wasn't aware of, had decided to leave his visiting son. He just didn't want to miss a night without going to the bar. Or maybe he just didn't want to be a father again. He'd got used to not being a father.

"Pass me another one here, will you Beery?" he shouted over, holding up his empty mug of beer.

It only took Barry a few seconds to get the drink for Jay. Barry loves serving his fellow beer lovers. Even if Sally the waitress were in, he would run quick drink-errands for his customers.

"Sally sick again, Beery?" asked Jay.

"Well. Can't say she ain't. Reckon you could fill in for her Jay, buddy?" he joked.

The mug was picked up from the table as soon as it was put on it. Jay took a hurried gulp as if the mug would disappear any second from his hand. He wiped his mouth with the sleeve of his maroon cardigan. The drink was strong on the tongue but light on the tummy. Jay loved how it tasted after keeping it a while in the mouth.

"That's the best thing you did. And the best that you will ever do, Beery, is opening up this bar. God bless you, son."

"Well," Barry liked to start all his sentences with *Well*. "Sure got that right old man!"

The sound of a glass smashing onto the floor broke the conversation. Barry hurried up to check it out. Jay didn't even bother to look at the direction of the attention. He resumed drinking his beer and could only hear Barry yelping and cursing. Barry wasn't keen on having people breaking his glasses and messing up his bar floor. "It's a waste that the modern civilisation can't afford," he'd say. Dropping a beer mug is the biggest crime one could commit in this skanky, little place. It would prompt an outrage involving a lot of verbal abuse, a shotgun being waved at the suspect, forcing him to wipe the floor and buy a round for the house. It has become such a tradition at the Triple B's that a song has been written for it.

"Well. You know the drill dumb ass? Get doin'" shouted the angry barman at his customer, who, without argument answered to Barry's demands.

Fingers were pointed and jokes were told at the poor glass-breaking victim as he bent on the floor, with his fat ass showing to his fellow beer junkies. And the song of 'Broken Beer Buddy' was sung.

> *Broken beer buddy*
> *You broke your pride and we're happy*
> *Get down on your knees and scrub the floor with honey*
> *And don't forget to give our main man his money*
> *And give us a round of beer to down in a hurry*
> *Broken beer buddy*

Jay waited for his free beer and soon after he downed it he departed the bar, thanking Barry for the drinks and the entertainment. He couldn't really stay any longer. He wanted to go back home.

It was getting late and Guy knew he should head back home by now. For the past couple of hours or so he'd been driving around Blossomville. He wanted to think things over. But soon enough found it hopeless. In fact it made him feel angrier than ever with his father. And he was annoyed at himself for forgetting about the photo he had on him of his father and the mayor. He also was distressed at what he had seen and felt in his parents' bedroom

He preferred focusing on the surroundings than have more of these disturbing crazy thoughts. He passed by his old high school. It was exactly the same, only they changed the sign. Now it's just plain black with white writing, it used to be gold plated with carved black writings.

He passed the public playground. A baseball field so ruined and wrecked stood in the silence and darkness of the night. It was in that particular field that he won that school game, which after he went to his dad and told him he'd be a pro ball player in the future. He played so well that day and he was very proud of himself. He wished his father were there to watch. Guy wanted to go out there and throw a couple of pitches for old time's sake.

He then passed through Tenth Avenue, which used to be famous for the variety of shops housed on both sides, which have all but one or two closed down. Only the barbershop was the same.

A very strange man used to work in that barbershop. At the beginning, little Guy was afraid of him. He, the barber, gave him the chills. His name was Leelu. He might have been Chinese, Guy never knew for sure. All the kids didn't want to bother him. They said bad things about him. Said that he would slash the throats of young children with his razor. When he first came to the area, Guy was about ten years old. By the age of thirteen, Guy became good friends with the foreign man.

They didn't talk with each other much—Leelu had a very thick, strange accent that was hard to understand—but had certain respect to each other and mutual understanding. Guy would tell him briefly of his aspirations of becoming a big ball player and how he would fight for this dream to come true. Leelu encouraged and praised his determination, but told him that one must not have dreams to make come true. They should not say that. He told him that dreams couldn't be reality. That dreams are dreams, and forever will remain such, no matter what you do. That they will remain a surreal image only in your mind. He told him that it is goals and objectives to achieve and fulfil that one must have. That to have a certain goal is even more accessible to reality than a dream, because deep within us, deep into our minds, we know that dreams are just fabrications of what we desire that we create to experience only in the unreal.

"And that is what makes dreams so unique." He told him

Guy didn't understand all of that back then, but now as he muses over it; it makes much sense to him. Dreams are exactly what they are…dreams.

Guy decided to stop at bar he drove past on his way back, as he was devilishly dying of thirst. It was small bar. He could see several cars parked outside. He parked beside them and went in. It was dark, the bar, almost as dark as outside. The few people inside looked dull and speechless. The place looked unfamiliar, but slowly, Guy began to recall it. He never entered it before because when he was here, he didn't drink. He was underage. But he heard a lot about it and how people would always hang there and drink all day and all night. He always wondered what it was like inside, but never admitted it to anyone.

He looked around and caught the attention of the individuals present; there were five of them, and they all fixed him with unwelcoming, cynical gazes. He was different. Not like them. He was young, they were old. He was thin, they were fat. He was handsome, they were ugly.

He stood at the bar and asked for a drink. The bartender, a funny looking chubby man, barely even looked at him as he offered him the drink. As Guy was about to turn, he crashed into a fat man holding three mugs of beer. The man dropped them all. Guy held on to his. The bartender stared in anger at Guy.

"Oh. Sorry," Guy said to the man, "sorry." The man just looked at him in disbelief. Guy was about to go on his way.

"Hey you!" shouted the bartender. "You blind, you dimwit? Now who do you think will clean up this mess?"

Guy, puzzled, looked around and then at the angry bartender. He shrugged and pouted. "You?"

"Well. Hell no, stupid bitch!" this brought laughs from the drunken men, "*You* will." He said, pointing a fat finger at the young man.

"I am sorry but I don't think so. Besides, that ugly fat gentleman bumped into me. It's *his* fault," he said nodding towards the other man, who seemed rather worried.

He headed to a table to have his drink, half of which was spilt on the floor. He took a couple of sips before the bartender came back with a shotgun.

"Well. You better clean this up or next thing you'll know is your head flying off of your neck!" he warned, with serious intent, or so it seemed to Guy.

"You are going kill me because I refused to clean up the mess that is supposed to be your responsibility. You will kill me and have my brains around this whole shit-hole?" he said, leaning back in his chair, trying to look tough and strong, ignorance flowing through him "Hmm. Who's going to clean that I wonder?"

Saying this, Guy, although a bit shaken, pulled a sarcastic smile.

The bartender loaded his shotgun. Guy stood up again, suddenly, feeling a weird urge to do something to this despicable fat man standing in front of him.

"Well," growled the bartender, "Do you know how many people I've had sweeping my messed up floor? Big men, men with pride and decency. It's about the beer, you see. You don't understand do you?" speaking through clenched teeth, the bartender then shouted with all his lungs, drawing the shotgun up at Guy "you will clean the floor you son of a fucking bitch!"

Guy as quick as lightening found himself pulling his 9mm pistol from his jacket pocket—which he had forgotten about up till that point—and fired one crazy shot, without even looking, all in a matter of no more than a second. It all happened in a flash.

The bullet landed in between the bartender's eyes.

He was dead before he hit the floor.

Chapter 17

▼

The corpse of the bar man lay still with the shotgun over his wobbly belly, a puddle of his own blood forming a perfect circle under his butchered head. Men's jaws dropped. All were dumbstruck. They all knew that Barry would never have fired. He only uses the shotgun to frighten people, but he never fired and he would have never done—matter of fact, everybody knows he never keeps his weapon loaded—Beery wouldn't kill a man.

No one expected the young stranger to pull a gun and shoot dead poor Barry.

No one spoke a word. And no one moved. They waited for the stranger's next move; which was to drink up the beer and depart the bar. He walked out, his gun in his hand, just like a cold-blooded murderer. He was indeed, for that moment, exactly that.

Having just killed a man for the first time, one would live through a mixture of terrible feelings. Fear is the most hideous of them. One would feel a rush, an urge to keep moving, running, to some safe place. But of course, nowhere would be safe, in a moment and a situation like this. If you killed a man, everything looks to you suspicious. You yourself become inconspicuous. Everything holds some degree of risk and hazard to the killer.

Slowly, you begin to realize that what you have done is something that will be within you for the rest of your life. Like a splinter in your head, you cannot shake it off. You cannot just run away and not get caught and be caught in its hellish webbing of remorse and guilt. This splinter will keep tearing you from within, tearing your brains, your heart, and your soul, driving you crazy.

Guy found a spot near a bunch of trees, off the main road, that he hid in for the night. He didn't know what to do anymore or what the next day would hold for him. Only a few weeks ago he was a regular guy, working a simple job. Now he is jobless, almost homeless and a murderer. And there is no hope of rectifying all of this. You moan and bitch about your stupid silly life, then when it goes away and is replaced with something more horrible, a living nightmare of some sort, you wish for it to all come back. This is how pitiful human beings are, thought Guy, they pray for a change, they wish for something, and then when it happens, it hits them that they have forgotten what kind of change they had wished and prayed for, good or bad.

He sat in his jalopy and leaned on the seat, pushing it back so he could lie, maybe to have some sleep. The night was silent. There were no sounds of passing cars or late-night trucks. No noises of beasts or midnight creatures of the wilderness. Nothing. Only silence.

It is in situations like this that one would want to convince himself that what has happened was just a dream. That he would wake up from it any minute and find himself out of breath, his heart pounding, relieved that the fear of this being a reality is gone. But Guy knows it is not a dream. It is real. Very real and it is inextricable. He knows because he can remember. He remembers pulling the trigger, and the fat bartender lying dead on the floor murdered and bloodied. Guy just realized that in a dream, one would not remember things. While you are dreaming you can't recall images from your past, whether real or unreal, in a dream there is only present, there is only the moment you are in.

So Guy sat there, mourning himself, weeping like a mother does over the loss of her young child. Reliving the infelicitous moment, and by doing so, bringing more pain and disgust and agony.

Just before dawn broke, Guy felt drowsy. He could not hold his eyes open any more. Reluctantly, he fell asleep.

When he woke up again, so suddenly, he gasped for air. He was shivering although it was not cold. His eyes were burning as though someone had sprinkled peppers on them. All his body was soaked with sweat. His heart was drumming. All these things were signs of an ugly, fearful, monstrous dream.

Although it was difficult for him to recollect the whole dream, Guy knew that it was terrible and that it had something to do with the events of the night before. It always happens, when a person has an overwhelming dream and wakes up in less time that a blink of an eye takes. The mind struggles to reform it, the dream, straight away and as time passes it becomes even harder to remember any of it. Guy has always struggled to simply just let dreams go, always focusing so hard to recreate them in his head, trying to construct them again, hoping that by doing so they would reassure his conscious, that it would help him make sure they were only just dreams and not reality, that he actually has some sort of power and control over them.

His stomach was making funny noises. It was screaming for food. Digesting itself in search for what it thrives for, throbbing and thriving and flipping and flopping. It made perfect harmonic sound with the birds of the early morning. He didn't have more than two hours sleep. The weather was heavily damp. Guy had to wipe clean his windshield, a thick layer of dew over it. He contemplated his fate, thinking what he should do, but he couldn't think of anything else than his stomach. That ought to be his first mission for the day. After a couple of twists, the ignition started. Soon after, he was on the road again, in search of someplace that would offer his screaming tummy some consolation

Aaron Minster woke up that morning in sheer exhilaration and satisfaction, because lying beside him was the girl of his dreams. He has been fantasizing about it day and night for so long, imagining how it would feel to have her in his arms, to kiss her and caress her and make love to her all through the night, to wake up to her perfect, bright face. It was worth the wait.

Last night was the greatest night of his life, as he made glorious love all night long with this girl; he finally had the night he almost gave up on having, since that fateful night they parted.

He didn't call her, didn't break up with her, and didn't even tell her what was going on. He simply disappeared after that glum night at his apartment, leaving her to find out for herself, to come up with her own conclusions. She herself never tried contacting him. She's not sure why she didn't. She'd let him go, blocked her feelings and swallowed her desires.

But when they met near the flower store yesterday, all of that—the turbulences and agonies and mistakes and hurt and pain—vanished without trace, and their true love for each other prevailed. It reigned like a little queen new to the throne. Aaron never saw again the woman he slept with the day he left Christina. He's been single ever since. He couldn't ever get Christina out of his mind. She stayed there, deep inside his heart and mind and soul.

Last night they worked things out, they talked about all the things they hated and all the stupid things they have done while apart from each other, and all that they needed to talk about. Christina even told him about her regrettable night with the stranger she met at the bar. She didn't remember how or why she got drunk; she didn't even remember the stranger's face. That upset Aaron a lot, but he was ready to forget and forgive. He'd made his own mistakes. He was ready to do anything for her and she for him too.

Yesterday, after their fated meeting, Aaron Minister and Christina Heywood had gone to the local hospital in Aaron's car to visit his sister, who had just had her first baby, a girl. He, Aaron, the 29-year old computer engineer, became an uncle.

His sister, Maryana, was married to one of the hospital's resident doctors for the past three years. This was their first child. One they have been wanting for a long time, but couldn't afford to have earlier, for reasons that only they knew.

They named the little baby girl Suzana. She was a beautiful and healthy child and Aaron was a very happy man indeed. He'd wanted to be there for Maryana, to be with her through the birth, but had been delayed a bit, by the rather fortunate, unexpected reunion with Christina. Maryana understood though; she appreciated him being there at all, in the absence of her husband.

Maryana's husband had been called to an emergency, surgery for an old man with cancer and a bad heart. Of course, the old man died after the 12-hour operation. It was hopeless, his case. Doctor Sam Dumin knew that. But still he, being the hard-working, determined doctor he was, gave it a try, answering his noble duty, even though it deprived him from witnessing the birth of his first child. He did all he could, for that patient, not giving up until the last minute, because that's the kind of man Doctor Sam Dumin is, the kind that Maryana had wanted to marry.

At the hospital's maternity section, in a white and blue room, Aaron held his little niece, Suzana, in his caring arms while Christina stood beside him, thinking how beautiful her lover looked with the baby and wondering how their children would look, certainly prettier. She shook off these dreamy thoughts with a smile on her face.

Aaron, still naked in bed, under the white, sex-stenched sheets, stared at Christina's pretty face, examined her straight nose, her large beautiful eyes, her smooth lips, as he ran the tips of his fingers over her silky soft skin. Her beauty was captivating; he felt his heart melting at that moment as she, with the most graceful of sleepy moves and cutest of yawns, began to wake. When she smiled at him his heart almost flew out of his chest.

"I had a dream," she told him, her voice angelic and sublime.

"A dream?" he said "Was I in it?"

"Unfortunately!"

"Unfortunately?"

"It wasn't a very nice dream."

Aaron lay on his belly beside her and started playing with her long, chestnut hair, "Do you want to tell me what it was?"

"No. Not really," she told him, even though she knew deep inside that she wanted to.

She liked sharing things, especially with Aaron. She missed having him around, knowing that he's right there beside her, listening to whatever she was going to say and share with him whenever she needed. But right then she had a bad feeling about this, about the dream she's had. She preferred keeping it to herself, for now at least.

It must have been their lucky day, though, because the weather was perfect. The sun brilliantly shining, spreading its golden rays through the fluffy white clouds. The weather in Okay was getting better and better each day as autumn kicked into full gear, keeping dry and warm with a sweet, cool breeze. It was time for them to get out of bed and get out of town for their usual early morning picnic.

"Been a while since we had one," said Aaron, as he kissed the forehead of the gorgeous creature in his bed, who was stretching her perfect, naked body, smiling and euphoric.

The sun was still making its way up, brightening the world. Little oak trees stood proud, their golden leaves thrown on both sides of the road, which looked to Guy different than the one he had passed on last night. Guy thought for a moment that he was going the wrong way. Things can look astoundingly different in the dark than in the light. They take on a different face.

There is a thin line between darkness and light that confuses a person.

As Guy drove down the road, he grew hungrier and hungrier. He couldn't recall a time when he was as hungry a man as he was then. Not even when his dad punished him as a little kid and locked him in the basement for countless hours. Yes, his father has been very harsh at times. He'd wanted to raise his kid in a way no one did before. Of course Morris received some blows as well. But Guy had the worst of it. Jay Kelton was a more aggressive father with his younger son, for reasons unknown to Guy to this day. He wished he had had that same thought earlier, so he could have asked his father. Another frustrating twist in his and his father's relationship.

As Guy, the murderer, spotted a mini-market ahead, he accelerated his speed. A pick-up van was getting closer and closer in front of him as he drove frantically, abiding to the needs of his stomach. The van was going slowly, or so it seemed to Guy, who hesitated before overtaking, slowing down, just to see a brown object being run over by the van and splintering into pink pieces. Guy, in one instinctive reflex, swerved, almost driving off the road and just missing ramming into a street lamp. After passing, Guy's mind was playing the scene through in slow motion. The brown object was a poor little cat; the pink pieces were its guts. It was a sickening sight, especially for a person who hasn't slept enough, who is dying of starvation, who had a frightening dream and who has killed a man the night before. Guy thought he was going to be sick, so he pulled over, but though he heaved, there wasn't anything within his weakened body to be thrown out. The poor cat, thought Guy as he got back on the road, though it probably didn't know what hit it. Strange for a man to think how a cat felt before it was hit and crushed by a car, feeling sorry for it, yet he hadn't even thought twice about the boy who was hit by a car and died equally gruesomely. People and animals aren't so different after all, he thought, as he felt a shiver in the center of his chest. Death. It seemed such an easy and simple thing. It doesn't take much. To kill and to die. It only takes a car…or a gun. As he was having all these disturbing thoughts about death, image-by-image the inchoate dream he had earlier began to come together.

He was on a beach. The water was blood-red. The sky was orange and the sun was white. Guy was standing alone, only for a moment. A figure of a man appeared some distance ahead of him, lying on the beach, near the bloody water. He was dead. Guy couldn't see this man's face. The sea, he realized, was colored by this man's blood. Then an angelic voice called on Guy, telling him that he had killed that man, that he had murdered him with his bare hands.

Murdered his father.

The voice was his mother's. Or perhaps it wasn't exactly hers but it represented her. Guy wasn't sure in the dream. There was static in the hollow air around him. Guy panicked. He screamed "NO!"

When he looked at his hands, he saw blood on them. They were bloody and had little black worms feeding on them. Another scream. The voice, which was supposed to be his mother's, tells him of the punishment children who kill their father get, to be eaten alive by the black worms of Hell

Then, without warning, the whole place turned black with only a gun floating in the center of it. Guy could feel that it, the gun, was being controlled by someone, or something, he couldn't identify or see. It was pointed at him now. He didn't move, or even attempt to.

Then a shot was fired and the bullet came as fast as light towards Guy, stopping suddenly right at his heart, just an inch away. Just then he realized he was completely naked standing there alone in the vast blackness.

The bullet, so ugly and vile, began, at a pace so slow it felt like a thousand years passed, to move towards Guy's heart, which was already hardly beating. The bullet was wrapped with barbed wire all around it. Its point was filled with little sharp edges. It touched his skin and began to rip its way into him and through his soft skin, very, very, very slowly, making him feel every curved sharp point injecting itself through his fragile flesh. It seemed to last forever. It pained him as nothing else ever did and probably never will. Just as the menacing bullet reached his heart, just when it was making its way through his heart's tissue, he woke up.

The mini-market he found, which was called 'Jo & Jo's Store', had almost everything a road-traveler would require: sandwiches, beer, soft drinks, burgers, fruit, chips, chocolate bars and even dirty magazines. Guy picked something from everything. Besides him, there was only one other young man doing his own shopping. He seemed healthy and affluent from the way he was dressed. What would a man like him be doing in such an area, and at this early time of the day? Guy was curious.

As he approached the counter, he remembered that he did not have any money. He was totally broke. There was no way that he could pay for everything he was planning on buying. But he needed to eat more than anything else now.

He placed his stuff at the counter.

"That'll be thirteen-forty-five," said the lady behind the counter, with her strong southern accent, after flipping through his groceries and punching buttons and numbers on the old teller.

"Ehm," he began, not knowing how to go around it. "I…"

"Yes?"

"Can you…Umm? Can you just put it on the bill…please?" that's the best he could come up with. He knew he sounded like an idiot.

"What bill?" she asked back, a frown on her face.

He sighed and rubbed his dry forehead.

"Look, I am going through hell here please work with me. Do something good in your life. I will take my stuff and come back later to pay you," he said nervously, "You see, I lost my wallet."

Of course he wasn't going to come back. He knew it, and she also knew it. Right then, he didn't look, or act, like the decent type who would return.

"Well, thankfully I haven't lost my mind enough to let you do that," She stared at him and gave him a stubborn look. He glanced to the left and then to the right. He looked up and then turned back at her.

"I'll be back!' he said, smiling falsely. Without thinking twice, Guy went out to the car and into the market again within seconds. The old lady noticed a change on her customer's face this time.

"Oh, did you find…?" unable to finish her sentence because Guy pulled out his gun and pointed it at her.

"Oh God!" she said in a low, hushed voice. "Oh lord!"

"Now, I am a very, very, very hungry person and I would like very much to have something to eat. And as you can see I am now a bit dangerous too. So stay still."

The lady froze on the spot. Her lips were wide apart and quivering. She almost wet herself, tears on their way down her cheeks from the corners of her eyes. She was frightened and scared; she thought she was going to have a heart attack. She'd never had a gun pointed at her before.

Guy was busy picking his stuff up off the counter when the well-dressed man popped up behind him.

"Ma'am are you all right?" he asked in a worried tone.

Guy turned to him quickly and pointed the gun at him. Shit. He completely forgot that there was another person inside.

"Take it easy, man. Take it easy."

"Step back," ordered Guy, waving his gun at the man. "I'll be gone now."

"I am afraid I can't let you do that,"

What's wrong with this guy? Guy thought. I am just taking some food. No money. Leave me be, he wanted to say. He would have even begged him to let him go. He was getting nervous and edgy, more so with every passing second. A sound drew Guy's attention to the lady at the counter. As he glanced at her, the man attempted to jump him and take the gun, but Guy turned back at him sooner than he thought and three sharp sounding bullets shot out of the barrel and into the man before anyone could take another breath.

Three in the chest.

He dropped back against a display shelf and fell down to the floor. There was smoke, and then there was a stiff body, and lots of blood.

Guy, in less than half a day, had killed two men.

Chapter 18

The road to Waterbed was the same that took you to Blossomville, only you have to take an exit five minutes before reaching the district. Aaron played his favorite Tonic record, Lemon Parade, singing along to the lyrics of *If you could only see*.

His 1973 Mustang Stingray fissured the air of the road in elegant fashion. It was his most valued possession, that car. He loved it more than anything in the whole wide world. He had bought it from an old man dying of cancer and a bad heart, almost two years ago. That old man had to sell the Mustang because he needed some money for an operation he was going to have, which wasn't a hundred percent success anyway, as his doctor had warned. But the old man figured he'd go for it anyway. He was lonely. No children. No wife. But it was still worth the try. He knew that one day very soon he was going to die.

Actually, Aaron Minister realized he loved Christina more than anything in the whole wide world. Now, Christina was his most valued possession.

The picnic basket was empty but of a little strawberry jam jar. They needed some things for their morning picnic The nearest and only store en route was one owned by a lovely old lady named Jo, and her husband, also known as Jo, hence the name of the store. Aaron and Christina had visited that same store many times before.

The drive was easy and quiet. Only two cars passed on the other side of the road, Christina counted. The sun was making its way up to the skies, still round and orange, and very bright. She rested her head on her lovers' shoulder and she sighed with comfort.

But the dream was still there in her head. Images from it still hovering around and flashing about her mind. She tried to ignore it but it just wouldn't evaporate, as with other dreams she'd had before.

In the dream she'd seen some person she thought she knew. He came and he took Aaron away from her while they were happy together, on some shore she couldn't recognize, where the water was red and the sky was orange. She tried to stop Aaron from going but he seemed relaxed and calm and wanted to go with that man. Hard as she tried, she could not recollect where she had seen him before, but he seemed unfriendly and that made her feel uneasy and worried.

When Aaron disappeared from her sight she waited and she waited and in the dream it seemed years and ages had passed while she waited for his return, but he didn't. And she knew he would never be back again. Not because he doesn't want to come back, but because he will never be able to. Because that man, that stranger that came and took him away, wasn't going to let him back.

Usually, Christina tried not to think about the dreams she had and tried to forget them as quick as she can once she woke up from them.

"Dreams are movies of the devil," her mother told her once, "They should be locked away and forgotten."

She looked up at Aaron, driving his car with joyous pride. "I am glad that I am beside you now." She said. For some reason she felt she was going to cry. Aaron turned to her and smacked a kiss on her soft wet lips

"Always."

He parked his '73 Mustang Stingray and went into the store. "Be gone five minutes," he told her. She said she'd take a pee; the lavatory was in a tiny room behind the store.

"I'll miss you," she told him, as his hand slipped away from hers slowly.

She watched him as he walked into the store, her heart already aching for him again. She suddenly had an absurd thought that she might never see him again. He's only right in there shopping for a few things, will be back in a few minutes, she chastised herself. Of course he will.

Christina, after doing her thing, stood in front of the mirror and sighed, then smiled. She had not felt this happy since they separated. Now she knew for sure that Aaron was what was missing from her life. That was why she kept having ugly dreams, been feeling lonely and sad and trivial. She could now see how their life would be together, in some lovely beach house, perhaps somewhere away from this town, someplace far from all the sloppiness and decedent lifestyle, with a cute big dog, maybe a couple of kids. Perfect. Just perfect. For that moment, the ugly dream she's had was gone and forgotten.

A thick thudding sound startled Christina from her beautiful daydreaming. Three times. She thought she heard a scream, but did not give it any serious thought. Probably some cracked up car or another. She looked at her wrist—watch, Aaron should be done shopping by now.

Christina walked back to the car, pulling her silky hair back as a lonesome tree caught her attention. She didn't recall seeing it before. Maybe she just didn't notice it. There was a trail of dirt in the air, which was left by a speeding car. The driver must've been in a hurry to be driving off like that. She couldn't see the car clearly through the dirt and the distance.

A crow stood on one of the trees' leafless branches. It flapped its wings and croaked and for a second it seemed to stare straight into Christina's eyes, then it looked toward the mini-market's door. Christina hesitantly looked as well; she saw a well-built man emerging from the market, holding a hunting rifle in his left hand. He looked at the car and returned back inside. Christina but picked up her steps and walked hastily.

Something was definitely wrong. It didn't look good. The big man, who Christina recognized as Jo, stood in shock in the center of the shop, trying to comfort the old lady. There were chip packs scattered over the floor. The lady was Mrs. Pinkerton, the shop owner. The big fella was her husband.

Mrs. Pinkerton was crying and shaking. Christina was stuck in a moment of disbelief, where was her lover, Aaron Minister? She couldn't think, her mind clogged with black clouds, and she told herself that it could not possibly be *him*, that man who appeared to be lying dead on the floor could not *possibly* be her lover.

Getting closer seemed an impossible task. Her heavy legs hardly carried her up to the scene. No one said a word for a long moment. There was only the sobbing of the old lady, hard and constant. Christina swallowed her tears and fears for a few more seconds then with watery eyes and trembling voice she said, "Call an ambulance. Call an ambulance." Her voice was so little it could barely be heard in the silent mini-market.

"No. No, it can't be. Oh god. Oh god," she wailed, kneeling down, a few inches away from the bloodied body of her smartly-dressed handsome lover. Hesitantly, while sitting on the floor, she tried reaching out for him, tried to touch him, but she was so scared. So terrified. Something inside her kept telling her he would wake up if she touched him, but reality told her touching him would mean she accepted the truth, that Aaron will never be with her ever again. He said he'd be gone for five minutes, now he's gone for good.

She prayed that it was just another bad dream. She tried to fight it but grief crept in. Another tragic loss; another abandonment. Grievance was her ally. Happiness was her enemy. Not because she chose it that way because she, like anyone else, cannot choose their destiny, or fate but because life is always harsh for someone.

It seems that that someone is always her.

The news about the men's deaths reached the Sheriff's office almost at the same time. The cleaner who called the cops, found Barry's body as soon as he entered the bar early the next morning. The blood beneath his body—his head to be exact—was the color of red wine, which indicated he had been dead quite some time. Early analysis from the coroner on the scene suggested it was more than six hours.

A couple of hours later, another murder was reported at a mini store on Highway 11. A young man shot another young man, killed him with three bullets in the chest. The caller, a man with a thick voice, told the police the gunman escaped in an old Caddie heading back towards town. There was a woman, he said, who seemed to know the victim, they were a couple who used to come quite often to the store, but it'd been a while since he'd seen them. She, he trailed, left the scene distraught.

The caller though seemed more upset about the food the gunman stole from the store. As well as the $10,000!

Chapter 19

He had to deliever yet another package for Barton. It was intolerable, but for now he had to put up with it. This time, the venue was different. Barton ordered him to go to an apartment in a ghost building, empty but for a tramp or two.

Patrick had never been to or seen such place before. The building was located on the corner of E-street and Bond in an area called Kingland. Well, there wasn't anything kingly or royal about this area for sure, Patrick thought to himself. But it was a crowded area, an area known for its cheap night bars and brothels.

As he climbed the stairs to the fifth floor, he saw things he had never seen and things he would never have wanted to see. The place smelt of rotten dead rats and urine, the walls colored with all sorts of graffiti and smeared with filth. He heard movement, then a weak voice asking him to give some money. It was a drunken young girl, skinny and petite, half naked, lying in the corner on the second floor stairs, who seemed to have a syringe stuck in her left arm. She was in her late teens, Patrick gathered. It was a distressing and depressing sight.

When he looked into the girl's eyes he saw nothing. There was only emptiness. The girl's eyes did not nictitate at all. Patrick was vexed by the image of her as she kept begging him for money. She also asked him if he had any drugs on him to spare. He could only shake his head and apologize.

"Go fuck yourself you worthless piece of shit." She shouted with all the strength left in her.

Patrick, eyes still crossed, turned away and headed up the stairs again. Never had he thought such miserable lives existed in this little town. And he thought he was miserable. He had heard the usual gossip and talk about the underground life, the hoodlums and thugs and homeless people suffering from famine, addiction and poorness, but up to this moment he was disassociated from it. He never expected to be confronted with it.

As he resumed climbing the stairs, he took another look at the girl. She seemed she could easily break if anyone had touched or moved her. The sight of her and this whole place gravely frightened him.

His steps were heavy and slow now. Every step he took he hated himself more and more, for accepting to do this, for actually contributing in producing such tragic consequences, such miseries. But he couldn't do anything. He couldn't because he knew what would happen to him and his girlfriend. Bad things. Barton would do very bad things to them.

"You will do this and you will do it my way and from now on you better listen to…" Barton told them, when he dropped in uninvited.

"No," Patrick cut him off.

"Let me finish please,"

"I said no, you scum! Get out. Now,"

"Well, well. Let's not talk to our boss like that shall we. Things could go pretty ugly for you two if you do," Barton said, his arrogance in full swing "See, you will obey me because if you don't, and if you think for a second that you can go tell the police or anything stupid like that, you will be the ones who will do the time for me and I will be out of it, just like a the rabbit out of the magician's hat!"

"You bastard!" Patrick abruptly said, his teeth clenched, fists ready to do some damage.

"Why so testy Patty? No one cares about what we do anyway. Just relax and enjoy the ride. Enjoy the pay-off," he told him, staring him in the eye. "This town is for the decedents. People just want to live and not think about all the shit going around in their undisturbed, pathetic lives. The question is, dear Patty boy, do you want to be one of them, or on top of them?" Barton said, a smile of malicious victory creeping over his blunt face.

It was obvious to Patrick and Mandy that this man couldn't be easily stopped, nor were they able to fight him. But it was his cockiness and over-confidence that nothing could harm him that angered Patrick the most.

Yes, if Barton were going to go down, he, Patrick, and even Mandy, would go down with him. They'd got their hands dirty. They knew too much and they are condoning it and going along with it, that in itself is a punishable crime.

When Patrick reached the drop-off point the first thing he noticed was faint voices coming from behind the door, probably three or four different ones. He knocked and the voices stopped. It was quiet. But he could still hear the moans of the drunken, drugged girl downstairs. Then there were several pairs of footsteps, though only one pair getting closer to the door, where Patrick stood silently, hearing nothing but his own breath. The anxiety he felt seemed to augment each time he made a "delivery".

This time it was as never before. At that very moment, Patrick thought of abandoning this mission. He thought he could simply drop the package and run down the stairs, take Mandy and straight out of town they go.

The knob clicked and the door was opened. A dark figure stood alone in the doorway. A powerful flashlight beaming from behind the figure made it impossible for Patrick to see his face and features. The man did not speak and only reached out his hand to Patrick. There was a long moment of reluctance before he handed a package he fully knew was full of drugs. The feelings of guilt deepened within him.

He was being drawn up to it, forced to do something he knew deep inside could result in nothing else but pain and agony to many people, including himself and the one person he loves. Should he keep finagling? Should he accept it and resume with this shameful practice? How would his life become? Would he be able to carry the weight? Will he forfeit his life because of it?

The man closed the door on Patrick without saying a word. Patrick stood in silence, not knowing weather his mission was completed or not. There was an unsettling feeling he hadn't felt before. There was fear. Something told him that it was too risky to stay. Just as he began to retreat towards the stairs, he heard loud voices. They were arguing. Then he heard quick, angry footsteps rushing towards the door. This time there were five figures emerging from the room like a herd heading for its afternoon meal.

The first thing Patrick noticed with these men was the guns in their hands. He was startled, an electric shock ran through his body, freezing him on the spot. He couldn't run, but managed to take one step backwards.

One of the thugs, although skinny, grabbed Patrick by the collar and almost lifted him from the ground. He was black and bald and wearing only his underwear. He smelled of rotten liquor. Patrick wasn't sure what was going on and couldn't think of a reason for the men to be upset, but he figured it was most certainly something bad and had to do with the package. He found himself praying to his lord to not have these ugly creatures hurt or kill him.

All five guns were pointed at his head.

"Who the fuck you think you're fucking with, you dick-less-fuck-face?" blurted the skinny man with a voice that sounded like a boxer-dog barking. He pressed his gun against Patrick's forehead. The latter closed his eyes and swallowed.

"You think you can fuck us up you fucking fool? We want our fucking stuff. This ain't the fucking deal!" Shouted the thug, ejecting sprinkles of saliva over his victim's face in doing so.

Patrick was still speechless. His mind failed to come up with a single word. One of the other men, a big muscular white thrash, drove his bricklike fist into Patrick's abdomen, making him give out a painful scream, which echoed in the filthy empty corridors of the crumbling building.

Still, his head couldn't make any sense to himself. Everything seemed unreal and his fear grew bigger every second. The pain from the punch made things even worse. He felt himself giving in slowly to the situation and the thought of getting killed was the only thing his mind was able to assimilate.

He couldn't hear what the thugs were saying to him anymore, but observed with quasi-sleepy eyes their moving lips and their hands waving the guns in his face.

The next thing he knew he was thrown down the stairs, feeling the edge of each step smashing into his ribs, back and head. He wondered when it would stop. Just before his head hit the wall on coming to a stop, the image of his beloved Mandy appeared to Patrick. He wished he were with her at home eating their favorite ice cream.

He landed next to the drunken skinny girl, unconscious. She looked at him, bruised and bleeding

"Welcome to the gutter club, sucker!"

A young rookie officer, whose name no one cared to know, took the description of the car in which the murderer escaped from the mini-market owner, who told the rookie he had been in the garage fixing a broken refrigerator when he heard the shots. He'd grabbed his rifle and ran to the rescue but saw the murderer already making his getaway. His wife, who saw the murderer's face very well, was in total shock and could not give a statement of the incident.

The officer took down all the required notes and details from the scene before the sheriff arrived. When asked what the murderer took from the store, Mr. Pinkerton said nearly ten thousand dollars, in addition to some foodstuff.

"Ten *thousand* dollars!?" repeated the rookie officer, "Are you sure of the amount Mr. Pinkerton?"

"Hell yeah! It was all our savings. We were planning to take it to the bank this very morning."

The officer took that down but thought that there was something fishy about it.

"You saying I'm lying?"

The officer ignored the question politely.

"When are we getting our money back?"

"Sir, it's too early to say anything or predict anything."

"Bullshit," whispered Mr. Pinkerton in disagreement, obviously getting agitated, and left the rookie officer standing alone in the market on the bloodied floor.

Sheriff Murray Markovic spent exactly ten minutes at each of the murder scenes and returned to his office by midday to not miss lunch at his favorite diner down town. He called Mayor Cunningham and filled him in with the details, which weren't much.

The Mayor was upset and almost yelled at the Sheriff over the phone. He demanded a quick explanation and an arrest of a suspect before sunset—not that he cared how the murders happened or what for, or even who did it.

"Get me someone so we can calm the people.' He told Markovic. "This is intolerable. I'm getting a lot of calls. You know how this fucked-up town is. Get me someone fast. I don't want the media start sniffing around."

The sheriff assured him not to worry about it and that it would be over very soon.

"For your own sake Markovic. For your own sake." The sheriff wasn't very pleased with the last remark at all, so he simply, scornfully, hung the phone up.

When Jay Kelton heard about the death of Barry the bar owner, he was very disappointed. He couldn't believe someone would kill that nice fella.

"God dammit!" he said "No beer tonight then. What a waste."

Guy Kelton sank his head in his hands while sitting on the bed in his apartment. He is in shock after the recent incidents, which have led him to kill two totally innocent individuals. It was beyond anything he thought he was capable of. The last twenty-four hours seemed to him more of an inundating series of parlous fictional spasms.

He sits and he thinks of the two lives he has taken and their families and friends, who he has now deprived of their loved ones. He, Guy Kelton, has averted all human emotions and feelings without the least of consideration in ending two lives from earthly existence. It did not give him strength; rather it gave him a mawkish sense of pompous anticipation. It seemed as if he were diluted by what he has done. Guy hoped that he had been dreaming all of this and that he would soon awake and things would be normal.

He stood and walked to the window, where he leaned his head out of it, supporting his elbows over the edge. Looking down, he saw little movement on the streets, a couple of passers-by and a few cars. A group of youngsters, gathered near a thrift shop on the opposite side of Guy's apartment building, were arguing over who's going to the liquor shop.

Feeling the warm midday sun over his expressionless face brought peace to his mind but it only lasted for less time than what he had hoped for, as his conscience resumed its rankling rarefaction. What made him buy the pistol in the first place was unknown to him. "There must be a reason," he thought. Guy tried reluctantly to figure it out. "Was I afraid? Did I get it to protect my self?" He asked himself. "But of whom and from what? What kindled me to equip myself with a weapon? What drove me to become a merciless murderer? There has to be a reason," he kept telling himself.

He drew himself away from the window and headed to the fridge but declined to open it. In the bathroom, he washed his face with cold water and looked at himself in the mirror. "I have become a murderer," he said to his reflection. "I am looking into the face of a murderer. I have never seen nor met a murderer before."

Suddenly he felt lonely, he shivered from fright and he trembled at the thought of what would happen to him. He then punched his right fist into the mirror hard with total abhorrence, breaking and shattering it to pieces. Contrary to what he expected, there was no blood. Only acute pain running from his knuckles through his whole body. He thought he ought to cry, but he couldn't. Everything was closing down on him. He struggled to breathe.

Guy picked up a large piece of broken glass and held it in his hand to gaze at its shape edges and curved lines for a moment. He pressed it against his wrist vein, closed his eyes and took a deep sigh. Every single cell in his weakened body began to tremble and shake as he, eyes still shut, squeezed harder on it and slid it quickly over his soft skin.

Guy clenched his teeth and opened his eyes wide simultaneously. A look at his wrist saw the damage was not fatal. The cut was short and not too deep, fortunately the vein wasn't reached. Awkwardly though, Guy found relief at the sight of his own blood oozing from the wound. Within seconds, the white bathroom sink was turned red as the tortured young man ran water over the bloodied wound.

It wasn't the first time he had thought of committing suicide. More than two years ago, when he was working at an auditing company as a desk receptionist, he thought of throwing himself from the window of the toilet of the company office in the fifth floor.

As he sat again on the edge of his rusty bed holding his wounded wrist, which he'd covered with a white cloth, he recalled the event, when he was so lost and depressed, after having too much trouble with his family and leaving them and after giving up hope of his life, of becoming something. He'd stared out the window, looking down to the bottom. He thought of the people who were going to see him first, thought of his mother, father and brother. "What would they have said about me?" He'd asked himself then. "Would they mention my death in newspapers?" At that time, two years ago, he failed to do it and again now he is not ready enough to do it.

But it was the circumstances that baffled him. How preposterous it seemed the motives behind killing himself two years ago, compared to right now, it was nothing. Why, he wondered, even though he had taken the lives of two strangers, is he not able to take his own? That is because life is sacred. It is the dearest thing one can treasure. Taking someone else's life would never be the same as killing oneself. There would always be motives and reasons and excuses. But to take your own life, one must be utterly mad and careless. One must be utterly and completely hopeless.

That day, Guy couldn't bring himself to end his life. He stepped back and broke down crying. After that incident he convinced himself that committing suicide would only bring more sorrow and pain, and torture the soul in the afterlife; that if one were to take his own life, their soul would be caged in purgatory for eternity. That's why it was difficult for Guy to do it then and now, because within him there was a fear of what would await him in the afterlife. He also thought of the aftermath, not in life, but after that, when his soul runs to its creator asking for forgiveness, for mercy.

"Our souls we do not own," his mother had told him as a boy "It is Gods' soul we have; we should protect it until it is back with its lord. We shall not harm it,"

"It has nothing to do with any of this. It's all in the head, all in the head", he kept repeating to himself.

Now, he is looking at his bleeding wrist, the cloth around it turning red. He feels a little tear dropping from his left eye. It falls down onto the cloth and mixes with the blood.

Chapter 20

The two killings became the talk of the town. Everyone talked about them, within their own little rooms, in their own small, shoddy houses, at their encapsulated offices, behind closed doors, between narrow walls. Everyone gave their own opinion and everyone formed their own stories and theories.

Word had it that the killer—a ruthless convict from out of town—was here to "straighten things out" with the mob. Which things would those be? No one dared say. Because in truth, there aren't any things to be straightened out, in truth there isn't a ruthless convict from out of town. How did such rumours start? But that's what small communities are brilliant at. They are masters in fabricating, manipulating and nullifying rumours that are utterly absurd and untrue, but are believed by the plurality of people so blindly as if they were the only truths there could have ever been.

Because of their lousy and austere lives, the people of Okay have become so numb they cannot differentiate between right and wrong. The two components seem to bear no value whatsoever to them, other than a misconception of community life. Their benevolence has been contaminated by the fear of encroachment. Every individual lives by his own little standards, inside his own little circle. Whatever is outside that little circle does not concern that individual. It makes life a lot easier to bear.

The last time the town got to talk so much about an incident was when Mr. Jacker was found stabbed and electrocuted in a lonesome alley almost three years ago. Nothing as peculiar had happened in Okay since then. It'd been as quiet as the early morning streets, if there was anything worth mentioning or controversy causing, the town officials made a good job being hush-hush about it. The truth remained unsaid, undiscovered.

Mr. Jacker, who nobody knew much about, left behind three little children to be fed and raised by his widow; a woman with a repulsive image but a great heart that no stranger gave the opportunity to be swayed by in their judgment of her.

Her parents had been more than happy to give their only daughter to the first man to propose. She wasn't getting any younger they said. She had to marry. Have children. She was thirty-eight years old. She had a terrible past in her relationships with men, which were few and far between. Something had to be arranged.

Jordan Jacker was a perfect fit. He was old, single, had money—not a lot but quite enough—and deeply needing to marry a woman. Her big brother hunted the old man down and offered him his sister as a wife.

"What's the catch?" asked the old man.

"There isn't one," he told him, "just get her out of our lives," The message couldn't be any clearer but the old man didn't mind at all.

They got married without a proper wedding, in some old forgotten church with no candles and no music. She wore a wedding gown that had been worn by at least a half dozen other brides before her. He wore a beige worn-out raincoat and a black bowler-hat.

Her parents weren't there, only her brother, and that was for no other reason than to ensure the wedding went ahead. She never saw her family again after that day, not because she didn't want to—despite all that they had done to her—but because they saw to it that she didn't.

They had children, three boys; the last was born after the peculiar death of his father.

Mr. Jacker wasn't a bad husband, in fact he made life easier on Shannon—that was what the old man used to call her though her real name was Amanda, but Jordan never liked that name so he began calling her Shannon.

"Because it's a good name," he would say, when asked, "It's a strong name."

One thing Shannon did not have a clue about was where her old got the money. It was a mystery to all.

"Soon I will die and it won't be much of a mystery then," he once told her "If news is for money today, it will be for free tomorrow". He seemed older than his age and more frail and weak when he said this. Shannon never understood what he meant by that.

Until this very day, it's still a mystery.

Leaning his back against the wall, and bending up his knees, Guy sat silently taking in all what had happened to him. With a little stick in his hand he began to play with the earth, making a scratching sound as he drew scrambled lines. It was too early in the morning for a lot of people to be walking around, so he'd decided to take a walk around the town's square.

It'd been three days since his murderous adventure. He had spent them all at his apartment. He did not go out at all, not even to get himself something to eat. Starvation had become an easy feeling for him over those three days; food meant nothing to him anymore apart from being the cause for his killing rampage.

Pickles, the doorman, came twice a day to check on him believing that Guy was very sick. On all occasions, Guy did not even make the effort to open the door for Pickles. He had locked the door so that nobody could come in forcibly. He wanted to be isolated from the outside world. Not even a single glance out the window. It was a closure he'd been waiting for, he knew that anytime they would come for him and take him away, and he wouldn't attempt to vindicate his crime. He wouldn't fight for his life because there was not much left to fight for. He condemned his own life to its doom the moment he pulled that trigger.

There were two tiny ants struggling to pick up a small piece of what looked to Guy like biscuit crumbs, each ant holding one of the ends, sensing its edges and shape with their little sensors. With a natural reaction, Guy directed the stick towards the two ants, aiming at the centre of one of them to kill it. It was normal human behaviour in seeing small insects, to kill them.

He felt that need automatically, but found himself, surprisingly enough, incapable of committing such an act. They were so innocent. They were too elfin and too tiny. They had nothing against him or against humanity, so why would he do such a terrible thing to them, why would he want to take their life away? All they are trying to do is get something to eat. That's their only purpose in life, not like humans who thrive for power and satisfaction.

He wondered how the ant would feel having her life taken without any reason but a man's boredom or emptiness. He tried to remember when was the last time he had killed an ant, but he could not. As far as he could recollect, he had never killed an ant—may be a cockroach every now and then, but never an ant. It was amusing to him to think that he had backed down every time he had thought of ending an ant's life, but never hesitated for a millisecond at killing the two innocent men.

He stared at the two ants walking hurriedly to take their catch of the day to their safe hole, happy for successfully completing their glorious expedition. Guy took the little stick in his hand away from their simple bodies, but just at that moment, a man's foot crushed onto the two ants in a flash. They were dead. Nothing left of them but crumbled little tiny organs.

It took him a moment to react as anger seeped into his veins; Guy cracked the stick in his hand into two pieces, stood up and ran after the passing man.

"Hey!" he yelled at him, "Hey you!"

The man, wearing a grey, striped suit, did not notice Guy's aggressive approach. He felt a stranger's hand over his shoulder and as he turned to look behind him, a crazy, powerful wild punch smashed into his face. He fell directly, face first, to the ground. The man started to make horrible, painful noises. Blood pouring out of his face, way too much blood for just a punch, thought Guy. But a look to his hand explained it all; the two broken pieces of the stick were jutting from his fist. The man tried to speak, but all that came out of his mouth were grunts and moans.

Guy stood over him, shocked and repulsed at the image. He looked around. A few people passed on the other side of the road, not giving any heed to the fallen man, but two young men were coming towards him. Realising what he had just done, Guy turned back towards his apartment building and started walking away. Not looking behind at all but still hearing the writhing man.

Their conversations have died out; their nights have become silent and their emotions frozen. The couple are now more estranged than ever, as if they were a thousand miles apart, yet their hearts are bound together by an unspoken undertaking. There was a threat in the air.

It'd been like this since Patrick returned that afternoon all bruised up from a delivery job. He had a cracked rib, bashed lip and large bruise on the back of his head. Mandy knew it had something to do with the illicit work they've been dragged into. He did not have to tell her.

Patrick took a couple of days off work, under the orders of his double-faced boss Barton.

"Stay off the streets for a little while, will you dear boy?" he told Patrick when he went up to him straight after the incident in the Kingland dump of a building.

Patrick, in temper, placing one hand on his rib cage and the other over his head to ease the pain, told Barton about what happened and demanded an explanation. "It was a simple misunderstanding," he told him, nothing to worry about.

His voice was calm and his face was expressionless so that it was difficult to determine whether what happened was planned for or really just an honest mistake, though Patrick knew there was nothing honest about that man.

Patrick, led in his actions by anger and despair, shouted that he would not be able to work anymore knowing that his life was in danger. It was not until later that he realised that he sounded, from what he had said, like an actual player. He had now become one of them.

"Let things calm down a bit." His devious smile was filled with mockery and power. The way Barton addressed him with these mobster-like metaphors, made Patrick jitter.

For some days they completely ignored the seriousness of their situation. They never mentioned their doings under Barton's reign. Patrick, being the person he is, tried coping with the circumstances as best he can. But for Mandy, her notion of the involvement of her lover, as well as her own, in this morose scheme destroyed her morality. She regretted pulling him into it when she told him about the job, she did not know that it would get this serious. She had been too preoccupied to even register the disappearance of her friend Christina Heywood. She'd not heard from her since the funeral.

They were sitting beside each other on the sofa at Patrick's place watching the morning news; Patrick holding a cold cup of coffee in his hands, with a cigarette butt dangling off his lips. It was an old stub. He did not smoke it today.

Mandy was playing with her hair and thinking about work when Sheriff Murray Markovic came on the news announcing the capture of the double-murderer. It was thanks to the massive effort of all the police force which brought such a ruthless killer to custody in a record time, bragged the Sheriff. "There is conclusive evidence, which will put this criminal behind bars for good", he said with a big shiny smile on his chubby face.

The building had a sense of fatuous ambience Guy had not noticed before. It was capricious in a foreign fashion, or so Guy reckoned it to be. His fist was still clinched and the two pieces of stick were still jutting out of it. Spots of blood from the stranger's face coloured his knuckles, the same knuckles he'd punched the mirror with, deep red. Passing Mrs. Jacker's apartment, Guy stood still for a moment. He drew closer and placed his ear against the door trying to overhear whatever was going on behind it. There was no sound, no voice. It was abnormally quiet.

It hit him hard that he never knew their names; he couldn't even recall one time that he had met with Mrs Jacker or her children or spoken with them. Concentrating hard to hear something, footsteps from above startled him. He resumed his ascent to his apartment at once, but with the same slow steps he'd always had. Pickles stopped him as he dragged his feet on the stairway.

"Oh, there you are Kel," he said, "You okay kiddo?"

Guy quickly tried to hide his hand away from the sight of the doorman.

"I got worried over you. Is everything alright?"

Guy passed him without even looking at his face, and without replying, taking a few more steps, "Heard about the murders? They got them their killer. It was all over the news just now," said Pickles.

Not only was Guy shocked by the revelation, he was frozen stiff; his blood ran cold through him. "How could they have captured the killer, while I am still here, free? Who have they got? How, when and why?" There were too many questions. Guy began to run, feeling his chest tightening. For that moment, the recent incident with the stranger across the street was completely forgotten.

He went straight to his bathroom and washed his hand. He found his pistol thrown on the sofa; how it got there he couldn't remember. What if Pickles had come in while he was away and saw it? It would have been a catastrophe. He felt a penetrating pain in his head, and running down through his body. How many people have now suffered from one man's reckless actions, nothing is making sense. Could some other stranger pay for his crimes? Is that fair? Guy certainly was not ready to accept such negation. The little bit of remaining sanity and his deadly, malicious phantom fought a battle of control over his tortured soul.

It was all paramount now, anger, depression, confusion, hate, sadness, and retribution, everything ugly and maddening. He couldn't think, his head and heart ached beyond belief. He ran straight out of his apartment again and out into the street.

The car was parked a few meters away from the building; he did not even try to get rid of it or even hide it. He started driving, unconsciously and aimlessly. He knew deep down inside that this must come to an end. How though he did not know. He was being driven to the edge, to the point where there is no return, to where things of hope and dreams do not exist. He drove fast, heading to the Green and West junction; his foot pushed harder on the flat accelerator.

He couldn't concentrate on anything, couldn't focus or think, as if he was riding a fresh-shot bullet, so fast and deadly and unstoppable. His eyes were drowning in tears. The roads were almost abandoned. He was driving so fast he could not do anything about it. He didn't care.

He closed his eyes. Felt the warmth of tears against his eyelids. And tried to recreate a beautiful image which would save him from all of this right now, one from his perfect daydreams of a perfect, beautiful life.

Suddenly, he felt things slowing down. The car was so slow. His heart was barely beating. Time almost came to a stop.

He opened his eyes again and looking ahead he saw a figure, which was not very clear to him. It was blurry but radiant. For a second he was certain he recognised it, like he had seen it before, perhaps in a dream. The figure was coming closer very slowly. Guy shook his head, hoping that if he did, it would pass. Since the killings, he hadn't had any of these sporadic twilight visions. In a flash, things went normal again and the speed gage was rock bottom. Before he knew it he hit the pavement of the little roundabout in the centre of the junction, the car jumped off, hitting a road sign and flipped, turning over seven times and then came to a halt.

Guy, during the whole accident, did not feel a thing. It was surreal. He couldn't think it was truly happening. He'd never been in an accident before. Could it be a dream? There were just flashes of colours and lights, sounds of metal cracking, glass shattering, rubber burning. It all happened in seconds, but seemed to last forever.

"Am I dead yet?" He thought before passing out.

A few minutes passed and he was awake. He got out of the car, stood, all covered in blood, in the middle of the road. No one was around. He looked over his body and saw his blood, it calmed him and he smiled at the sight. He was dizzy, felt his mind slipping before falling down on his knees.

He lay on the ground, still no one passed by. It was late, very late. He looked up the sky. Stars, oh how much he loved stars, glowing and shining. Lighting the dark blue sky. But wait, it was early morning, how could there be stars, how could it be so dark?

"Beautiful," he whispered to the stars, and his eyes started to shut slowly; there was movement around him, people, noises and voices. His heart was beating slower and slower, he breathed air saturated with the smell of oil and rubber and blood.

His eyes were fully closed now. He rested. No thoughts, no memories. His whole life did not flash before his eyes.

He just went to sleep.

After moments of pitch black, which did not seem to be anything like time, Guy felt alive again. He saw people carrying a casket; among those people where his father, his brother, his mother, and old friends who he had not seen since school days.

"What's happening?" he asked, not certain if anyone could hear him. He got closer to the congregation, they were crying and weeping and wailing. He called them, shouted. No reply, no one even noticed him there.

It was a cemetery, he realized. The sky was tainted dark grey and the air was still and damp. He got even closer. There was a tombstone; it read:

GUY JAY KELTON 1980-2004
PHLEGMATIC SON & MURDERER.

"No, that can't be," he said, "I am here. Father, look at me. I am not dead!" he cried out but to no avail. He was a ghost. He was dead, to them. His heart beat violently, he couldn't breathe, and the air was sucked out and away from him.

Everything around him started to fade into black then, the grave, the people, and the cemetery…the sky. He was alone, again, standing in darkness, not knowing what to do now.

Now that he is dead.

Suddenly, there was a white ceiling and bright lights. His eyes were opened. Moving them around, he saw whiteness all around, white bed, white floor and white walls.

"Where am I?" he said, more to himself "What's going on?"

He heard voices coming from behind the white curtains. He couldn't understand what they were saying. A young woman dressed in white came in.

"Oh, sweet lord! Doctor Dumin, our patient has finally awakened, come quickly!" said the woman, in apparent excitement.

"What? Doctor? Is that…oh it must be,"

"Let me see. How are you son? How are you feeling?" said the doctor, a man with receding hair and clean face, wearing thin glasses and a thin goatee. He looked into the patient's eyes and checked his vitals.

"He is in aftershock, but doing remarkably well by the looks of it," he said "Don't worry young man, you're in good hands," he told him, giving a reassuring smile.

Guy realised that he couldn't recall anything; he couldn't remember a single thing about what might have happened to him. What was all of this? Another dream? He was trying to focus and concentrate, but the nurse was distracting him with her medical tests. He did not know anything, anything at all. It was all gone.

"Who am I, woman?" He asked.

"Well, I don't know! Why don't you tell me?" she replied, she was sweet looking, not pretty, just sweet.

A long pause.

He was inspecting the surroundings in absolute bewilderment, as if he had never seen such a place before in his life. After failing to recall what had happened or anything at all of his life, he turned to the nurse and asked in anxiety:

"What happened? Why am I here? Please tell me, I must know,"

"Just lay back and relax young man. Never worry yourself now. Patience, honey, it will be all over soon."

What will be over? He thought.

"Isn't it over already? Am I not dead yet?" he said, his face was one of total oblivion and confusion.

Chapter 21

▼

It took a while but not as long as he first thought it might do. Within twenty-four hours he had completely regained his consciousness and his life. Bit by bit, hour by hour, his memories resurfaced and he realised who he was, what had happened and what he had done.

Once he did, he felt he couldn't stay in the hospital for one more minute. He had to get out. He felt surprisingly good, his injuries weren't as bad as they probably should have been, mostly cuts and bruises, nothing serious. He had heard the nurse say that it was a miracle how he had survived the crash. They were still struggling to find out who he was, they couldn't find any files in the hospital records for him nor find any documents on him. He knew he had to leave before they did. At dawn, just when the hospital's population was still snoring, he gathered his strength. He put on his torn clothes, which were kept in a plastic bag in a cupboard next to his bed, and grabbed all the painkillers he could lay his hands on, and escaped unnoticed.

Something, some sort of mystique power, forced them, unknowingly, to head to Marco's Bar.

Guy Kelton and Patrick Roymint were both thinking of their bizarre meeting a few weeks back. It seemed like yesterday but it was not. Many things had happened to both men during that time, and it left them with no time or the desire to retake on the events which accompanied that meeting—prior, during or after it. To them it all died and ended as soon as they walked out from the bar that night.

Now, however, they are returning once again. For what, the two men could not understand. It seemed natural to the two; perhaps for need of nostalgic purposes, to reinvent something they both doubted in life, the recreation of a rational existence some way or the other. Perhaps they just wanted to have a drink.

The day was just beginning to fade away, the orange sun already gone in its own twilight. The chill of early winter awakened their numb senses. They walked, dragging the disappointments of their recent mingling misfortunes along, both bowing their heads to the ground, drowned into thoughts of subdued mortification.

As they met at the door, neither looked up at the other. There was a moment of hesitation as each waited for the other to enter before one made the first move. Both thought to themselves how absurd such situations are, each trying to be prudent and polite

The same band was playing the same music at the back of the room. The atmosphere inside the bar was gloomy and poorly lit as ever. The air was thick with smoke and intoxicated with the smell of booze. Young crude men and women, some were jigging to the bad music, others were looking manic by the thrill of getting drunk, were scattered across the vicinity. Like two dancers in a ballet, the men walked along towards the same seats they occupied on their previous meeting, still ignoring the presence of each other. They were also wearing the same clothes, Patrick in blue old Levi jeans, black t-shirt and brown-leather jacket and Guy with pale blue jumper over khaki pants.

The only difference in their looks now was the bruises and injuries they'd gained.

For a long moment, they sat silently, awkwardly staring at their hands and playing with their fingers waiting, anticipating. Flashes of the unusual dreams and visions—if they could be called such—that Guy had in the past weeks came to his mind against his will. The dream with the king and his brother, the old man and the big gate, his mother's room, the bloody beach, the figure before the crash, all these had to have a meaning. They must.

But then again, there were all these embittering incidents in which he became a merciless, humanity-consuming monster. Taking the life away from others, easily incited and driven to act out of nemesis. He has murdered two men and deformed the face of another. What does *that* mean? Could the two be connected? Is there reason between his dream-like visions and his actions, or is he simply going mad?

His life is slipping away from him. He is losing all that he is—which was not much in the first place but is now all he wants—in what seems to him now as more of a reclusive punishment, with no respite, to his self denial and refusal to the life he has been given, creating an indefinite labyrinth designed by explicit consequences, leading to an infinite and inescapable prairie filled with sharp needles instead of green grass where he is to roam for ever.

One question remained in the back of his head, stinging like a splinter, why is he still alive? Why hadn't he died in that crash? Why is he still a free man, sitting here in a bar, trying to have a normal drink like normal people, when he instead should have been rotting in a prison cell?

His injuries were bitterly painful. He wondered if it was a smart idea to leave the hospital like he did. What does it matter? He winced as he bit down the stinging pain, taking a few more tablets.

Patrick however was more concerned about his dilemma with the mob. How on earth would he be able to escape them? To detract himself from all the sins he has committed and helped doing? Would god—if he ever existed—forgive him? But more importantly would he forgive himself? He struggled to accept the fact that one simple decision he took has brought him to the state he's in now.

The rope of their thoughts was cut by the thick voice of the chubby gum-chewing waitress, "Oh, you two again?" she said with a tone of mundane mockery.

They hesitantly peeked at each other, sliding their eyes to the corner and slowly turning their faces. The waitress was standing in between them from behind, "What can I get you?" She asked resentfully.

Their faces stayed expressionless for a second, before they were taken by the unexpected surprise. They did not say a single word to each other. There was a long pause between the three alienated persons, as cheap, shambolic jazz, travelled through the narrow spaces of the bar.

"Look," she stressed, obviously running out of patience when the two didn't reply "Do you want something or not?" waving her hands around.

"The same," they simultaneously said, expecting her to remember what they had the last time. Of course she did.

What is he doing here? Both asked themselves mentally. They wondered where the other had been all this time and what he'd been up to? They wondered if the other ever thought about that previous meeting, here at this very place?

Finally the odd silence was broken. It was Patrick who spoke. He said, "You had an accident."

Guy was not sure whether he was telling him that or asking. He decided it was a statement, either way he could not but agree, shaking his head and touching the bandage placed at the left corner of his forehead with the tips of his fingers. It did not feel like he almost lost his life. There were too many questions to be asked, too many gaps to be filled. Their eyes were of aggravated anticipation. Yet somehow they both knew that the answers to all their questions and the solutions to their dilemmas lay in one another.

Chapter 22

Yearning for solace never works. In grief there is nothing but heartache. Losing someone you care about and love always leaves a black empty hole in the centre of your soul. A scornful hole, no matter how much one would want to conceal it and be discreet about it, it takes another person just to look into their face to know the severity of the pain that loss has inflected upon them. There would be a sense of despair, of doom and anger in their aura. There would be signs of restless pain in their eyes. Their breath would be heavy and gelled.

Christina Heywood had been feeling none of this. The sight of her rekindled lover laying slain over the floor of some rusty little store, on some abandoned road on one beautiful early morning, wretched her every flame, every sparkle, of a new hope. A hope that was relinquished, vandalised, victimised…assassinated, by whom? And *for what?*

She had subsided everything and suppressed her emotions into the back of her head. She was so traumatised, so shell-shocked, that she couldn't feel anything anymore. Life seemed to her vague and pointless. The optimistic way she'd been looking at it had dramatically changed, had gone the moment she walked into the store and saw the one thing she never could have contemplated.

The past few days Christina spent absorbing the elements that led to her current condition, the events which have brought her to this point. Her losing her stable job, the demise of her mother, the murder of her reunited lover…How can life go so wrong for someone in such a short time? Everything happens for a reason they say. Christina could not come up with a single one for all those things.

One thing she could not ignore, one thing this feeble woman could not forget, was a dream, a visionary dream.

She had seen her lover being taken away by a stranger, lured to the unknown in the hands of an intruder. She had seen that just hours before her Aaron was shot three times in the chest by some ruthless bandit. Was it destiny? Or was Aaron just there at the wrong time and place? But that vision, that dream, it was a sign, a heavenly statement, a warning. Where do these visions come from and why?

She was so confused by the overwhelming complexity of the matter. Visions are just meaningless dreams until they are realized, and when they are it would always be too late to act in order to avoid it. It is part of our destiny, our fate, which is why it is impossible for us to comprehend the gravity of this vision, this dream, before it brings its toll on us. We must accept them as messages from the heavens above, so that we either feel more guilt about what has happened, or feel luckier to have been prepared for such devastating results, as more often than not, these visions are grievous.

Just now, Christina recalled the many times she had had visions such as these, but never gave them heed. Since she was a little child, she had visions, of things that would affect her deeply, come to think of it, she now remembered the dream-visions she had just before she was fired from her job, and just before her mother had died, and even just before her father left that day and never returned again. But she always ignored them, locking them deep down inside her mind.

She had spent most of her time now at her mother's house, carrying out the mundane daily activities of housekeeping. Something she had not been used to when her mother was around. Even with her unstable health, Christina's mother kept sweeping the floor, cooking the meals and washing the clothes. She never seemed to grow tired of doing them. She loved serving her child. She tried to provide her with all she wanted, but knew that there was something missing. She knew that her little child was struggling to keep away the image of her father from her life. It was never easy for Natalie to be the father and mother of her only child. And Christina realised that as well, as a child and as an adult.

In the mornings she made breakfast for two, watered the dying plants in the front porch, swept the floors and washed her and her dead mother's clothes. In the afternoons she went out walking in the market, at the park or circled aimlessly round the neighbourhoods, looking spuriously benignant to stranger's eyes. During the night all that she could ever think of was her father. If he were still alive, he would be the only thing she got. The only family and the only person she cares about and loves. Yes, she still loves him. Even though he had left her as a child, when she needed him to be around the most, and never returned. She needed him when she was a child, and she needs him now. She cried and cried so bitterly alone in the night, praying to heaven that her father would walk back through the same door he walked out twenty years ago, holding her and folding his arms around her, sitting her head on his chest and telling her that things will be fine and that the roses will prosper and glitter once again.

This afternoon, she decided to spend one of her quiet days at the park. She visited the bookstore first. The Asian shopkeeper greeted her with pleasure, told her that it's been a while since her last visit. "Yes, its been quite a while," she replied, "and its been a while since I last read an enjoyable book." She nodded a greeting and went on her errand, to discover a book which would induce many untouched melodious memories.

She walked between the large shelves where old and new books were stacked together. Her eyes searching for some sort of a mark, a sign that would lead her to the right book that matched her state of mind and mood.

Reading, to Christina, is the food of the soul. Reading fiction to be exact. She bought her first paperback novel when she was a young pupil at school—she had never even attempted to show the slightest of interest in a book before that—but all of a sudden she started reading, not children's books about fairytales and giant wizards, but adult novels, about sinful romance and the drama of life. The true reason behind that was, to her, still unclear. Something unpredictably eager and wary within her was unleashed. She was eleven then.

That first book was about an ageing legendary baseball player who had to come to terms with his retirement. She read that novel and she fell in love. Because of that book she managed to live someone else's dream, even though for a short period, of being a legendary sportsman. She had experienced the rush and excitement of competition, of the sweet joy of victory. She had the love of her life.

The surge of feelings and the stirring emotions she had experienced while reading that book, were more than just captivating. Reading that book gave her the opportunity to live another life, and that's what reading was all about, she presumed. To experience the things that we would not get the opportunity to have the pleasure of experiencing in our lifetime and under the circumstances of our current lives.

She had read so many novels and lived so many lives. She had fought monstrous Norman tribes along with the Viking warriors, she had solved mysterious crimes and brought justice to the world, she had felt the fear of war as she dug tunnels under the French soil, She had felt the joy of love, felt life as she never had before.

It had become an obsession; more so an element of which her soul was kindled by, a way for her to understand the world and life's mysteries. To read is to shun yourself from the world you live in and fly into a world that is so foreign to your regular senses, to indulge yourself in mental masturbation. By reading we expose our emotions and share our compassion, as we turn each page and rattle our eyes through the thin lines and small fat letters. What makes reading even more gratifying and fascinating is the nexus of human emotions.

Her mother never asked what books she read as a child, she trusted her taste and she knew that she must give her the freedom to at least choose the way she wanted to swim into oblivion.

They say "Don't judge a book by its cover" That could be half true. You see, no matter how hard we try to deny it, the cover says almost everything about the book simply because it's the first thing that your eyes come upon. It's part of human behaviour. It's the instinct we are born with. To judge things by the way they look, by their appearance. Christina acknowledged that. But the pattern in which such judgement is made, she reckoned, differs from one person to another.

When she chooses a book, she takes her time. To her it is an art in its own, one that any serious book-reader must master. It's not just about who wrote it, what it is about and what it represents. A book-reader must acknowledge the existence of this book. You have to feel the book, running your fingers over it, feeling the smooth freshness of its papers, or perhaps its rough gleeful cover. We have to listen to them. Yes, books. They talk. We have to listen to what they say to us. Some tell us to pick them up and flip through them, or urge us to open the first page and read its first few lines. Some others tell us to turn our backs and leave them alone on the dusty shelves or would just stare back at our bewildered faces in an attempt to seduce us.

Seeing all the books, waiting for someone to divulge into their deep secrets, encourages Christina's hunger. She desires to devour all of them, but realises that, even if she were to live until the end of the world, she would not succeed in that.

In a heap of separated books placed beside one of the stores' reading desks, she found the desired book. It was one about a single mother trying to raise her child in the best possible way in a community full of diminished souls and how that mother had to become what she would never want her child to see her be, to come to terms with life. Christina never cared to read the books of one particular author, because she disliked reading the same style…there are so many books and so many authors, why should some be preferred to others just because of a name?

She picked the book up and headed to the Asian at the counter, whose nametag simply said KUMAR.

"Ahh, a nice book you select missus Heywood," he said with his thick Indian accent as he placed the book in a small plastic bag. "I'm sure you like."

She thanked him, paying him and taking the paper-bag from the smiling Kumar.

As she walked in slow steps, still inspecting the books on both of her sides, Kumar called after her, "Hope see you soon. Come back quick!"

Emerging from the bookstore, Christina almost bumped into a passing stranger. She came to a sudden halt, to avoid a collision, looking at the man strolling on his way, not seeming to notice her coming out of the bookstore. At that moment, as Christina stared at the man's broad shoulders, she recognised a face, the face of another man coming towards her. She struggled with utmost difficulty to draw the picture of that man's face from her memory. She knew beyond any doubt that she had seen that face somewhere before. But where?

Coming closer, the man, who had both hands inserted into his trousers pockets, seemed lost and confused, distant and separated from the world around. She surprised herself feeling a bit of pity towards this man.

Then it just struck her. Her heart almost stopped beating at this paralysing revelation. She remembered where she had seen that face before. She could not have forgotten it; it was there atrophied in her brain cells. Anger, fear, disbelief, an overwhelming surge of emotions rushed through her.

She froze.

That face was the face of the man who had come in her dream and taken her lover away from her.

It was the face of Aaron Minster's killer.

Chapter 23

The case was closed. The police had themselves a suspect. He did not have an alibi, he had motive—according to the Sheriff—and he had a previous criminal record for assault and robbery. Perfect fit. As for clues, there were none at the time, probably there would never be. But in Okay's justice system, that is not necessary.

Sheriff Markovic didn't want to waste more of his time on this case and he wanted to get it over with soon. More importantly for him, he wanted the Mayor to get off his back. The man they apprehended was some neglected street beggar who they picked from his shack in Kingland. There was a lot of controversy going on about the case, but nothing that the self-imposed heroic Sheriff was concerned about. He wanted to look good, keep a good record of crime fighting, regardless how it would affect others. His and the mayor's obsession with grandeur and power overlapped justice and fairness. Nobody asked who poor John Doe was, or why he was aggressively dragged out of his so-called house while he was sleeping on the street. Nobody wanted or dared to question the Sheriff's or the Mayor's credibility and decisions. They believed in them blindly.

The rookie officer who had been first to the store murder scene, was not convinced with the way the Sheriff dealt with the case. He felt that there were many loose ends that needed to be tightened. There were still many questions left unanswered, but no one dared ask them.

He'd become an officer only three months ago, and this was the first case he had been involved in, not that there were many in the first place. He could not cope with the common attitude in the department, the carelessness and not-giving-a-damn-about-what-we-do attitude. He'd been struggling to remain silent and not crack up from feeling guilty about not doing something about all of this. He tried to convince himself that this was how real police business is done, that he would get accustomed to it soon.

But he couldn't. He couldn't simply turn his back just like all the others; even the good men of Okay had been turning their backs far too long. He wasn't raised like that, he couldn't not care, couldn't ignore injustice.

Officer Randy Challenge was raised by God-fearing parents, with his two brothers and two sisters, in their humble house by the river. His father was a farmer, who struggled in his profession because it was a dying one due to the weather in Okay growing worse and worse every season. Crops were dying. Cattle were dehydrating. All other farmers in the area either gave up the business or moved away. But it was the determination of his father, and strength of his mother, that made him the man he is today. And he is proud of it. He only wished others could see that in him.

The first thing the tall, thin rookie did in his own quest to solve this double murder was to visit the Pinkertons. How Sheriff Markovic was so certain that the same person committed the two murders in the first place was a mystery on its own.

That was the first question Randy wanted to find an answer to.

The weather was pleasant with warm sunshine and slow frequent waves of cool breeze. The sky was clear. Autumn was in full swing as was evident through the yellow and golden leaves falling off trees and flying about.

Randy parked his car in the empty dirt park in front of the mini-mart; he stepped out and for a moment inspected the surroundings. To the left there was a deserted gas station, which seemed ready to collapse at the slightest of gusts, and to the right there was a red, rusted water tank, standing on thin metallic poles. It also seemed ready to collapse at the slightest of gusts.

Randy stared at the sign saying 'Jo & Jo's Store', and with a sigh began walking towards it.

As soon as he entered the store, the young rookie officer was met by the big Mr. Pinkerton, who obviously remembered him from the day of the murder, with curious eyes. "Found the money yet, have you?" he asked straight away. Randy ignored the question by rotating his eyes around the store, looking for some sort of previously overlooked evidence. Mr. Pinkerton frowned at this.

"I need to see your wife, Mr. Pinkerton," he said.

Mr. Pinkerton frowned, walked back behind the counter, with slow heavy steps, and glanced at the officer's feet. Randy in turn looked down and found that he was standing over the dried bloodstain of the late Aaron Minister.

He took one step back.

"I need to ask her a few questions, sir," he added.

There was reluctance, and Randy sensed that the guy wasn't pleased with the idea of having himself, looking fresh out of the Academy, questioning his ailing wife.

"She's in the back. The second room to your left," he said, "She is still sick. What more do you want from her?"

But the officer was already on his way, not paying much attention to what was being said to him. When Mr. Pinkerton followed, the officer turned to him and halted him with the palm of his hand.

"You'll be of better use where you are Mr. Pinkerton." He told him.

After less than five minutes, Officer Randy Challenge emerged from the room wearing a confused expression. Putting on his hat, he traveled with slow steps towards the exit, his eyes gazing at the wooden floor.

"What about our money?" yelled the man behind the counter; seemingly not caring about what had gone between his wife and the officer.

But again there was no reply.

John Pinkerton had to be in town to settle the food supplies orders, so he left as soon as the "useless" officer was gone.

In the last week of each month, Mr. Pinkerton visited Karmafoods, their suppliers, to place new orders and every month there seemed to be a problem with the order; a delay in this or a delay in that, some stuff missing, confusion about the fees. What could be done about it? Nothing. The company is the best and the only.

Mr. Pinkerton married Mrs. Pinkerton, almost ten years older than him, because they needed each other. She needed a man to look after her and protect her, and he needed a woman to serve him like the mother he lost as a young child. Helpful to the cause was that they'd known each other for a very long time.

They lived with each other for a while before they agreed that it would be best for the both of them that they get married.

Mrs. Pinkerton inherited the shop from her father, who'd died in a freak accident with a cat! He'd been almost eighty years of age when he died. One day he'd been sitting in his usual rocking chair outside the shop, near the gas station, when a hideous ugly skinny cat came at him. He did not notice it until it started licking his exposed lower leg. He, with his paranoid mind, thought a scorpion had bit him and jumped crazily up from the chair, just to trip on the cat's tail, causing much panic to both himself and the cat, making the latter scream out painfully. The old man then tripped and fell over the cat, landing on its open mouth. It's sharp long teeth ripped through his neck, easily slicing open his soft, thin skin and cutting an artery.

He died within seconds.

The cat escaped with broken teeth.

No one quite believed the story, but his daughter stuck to it, saying that stranger things can happen in life, and they certainly do. Her brother and sister thought that their sibling was as crazy as their old father, and they were more than glad to be dropped from their fathers will. The shop was already heavy with several mortgages, loans and debt.

Both husband and wife struggled for many years to stand on their feet without the help of anyone. "In memory of the old man," kept saying Mrs. Pinkerton, "we must keep it going".

John had the usual fight with the people at Karmafoods and walked out with nothing better than he usually got. He decided he needed to eat some of the city food; he was growing tired of his wife's cooking. He headed to the nearest steakhouse, because Mrs. Pinkerton certainly did not make the best steak in town.

He tried to make the most of each trip each month, because he and his wife didn't go out on social occasions together much, one reason being that recently Mr. Pinkerton was becoming more embarrassed by his older wife, who didn't like the modern ways of living anyway.

Once, he'd gotten into a lot of trouble when he decided to visit one of the town's main nightclubs, a place known as 'The Pyrope'. He'd taken his only proper suit, placed it in a plastic bag and hidden it from his wife. He was curious, and wanted to see what those places were all about.

He got in easily, to his own surprise. He was nervous, and seeing the stack of people, hearing the loud music, and inhaling the smoke, made things even worse. There were women with barely a piece of cloth or two covering their bodies, there were half-naked ladies dancing like mad all over the place, and there were men who seemed to be sedated or drugged and not aware of what they were doing.

He walked about, feeling exacerbated, stunned, excited, reached the bar and got himself a drink, which he gulped down in one take. When the bartender was about to refill his glass, he stopped her and shook his head no.

"I can't afford another one," he said, with a nervous smile.

"Then what are you doing here honey?"

The bartender was a young girl, maybe in her early twenties, with piercings on her ears, bottom lip, tongue, and left eyebrow. She wore her purple hair as short as a boy's.

She didn't seem very friendly. At least not with me, he thought. She nodded at one of the huge bouncers, who was more than pleased to answer the call.

"Go on pal. Beat it." He yelled at a now shaky Mr. Pinkerton with his booming voice, flexing his muscles at him. The bouncer then grabbed him by the arm and started pulling him out of the place. John almost stumbled and fell. Reaching a hand to keep himself balanced, his misfortune brought that hand over one of the almost-naked women's chests.

"You freak!" she screamed, "Fucking perv!"

That prompted the heavy bouncer to drag him even rougher and to give him a couple of kicks, and another bouncer—this one seemed bigger and more aggressive—joined in.

Mr. Pinkerton was thankful that he got out of that place with no permanent damage, and no visible bruises, which his wife would've questioned. He swore never again to step inside such a place.

Walking down Main Avenue towards the city center, with a smile on his face and an empty tummy to fill with juicy steak, Mr. Pinkerton passed an old man sitting on an old, backless chair reading the day's newspaper.

A front-page photograph caught his attention; it seemed to be of a car accident. He did not know why, but he thought he had seen it before, like in some sort of dream or other.

The headline read: *'Young man escapes fatal crash…then disappears!'* Pinkerton realized it was the car in that photograph, despite being smashed pretty badly, that had caught his attention; he recognized it because it was rare, so rare, he reckoned, the police should not have had a problem finding it. It was the car in which, whoever it was, sped off after the shooting at their mini-market.

It was the killer's car.

Chapter 24

▼

Was there hesitation? Yes, there was. Was there fear? Yes, of course there was. But it had to be done. To be able to end this crazy situation he was in, it had to be done. But could he do it? No, certainly not. Because it had to be done by someone who knew what he was doing, someone who had done something like it before, or someone crazy enough to act on it.

Someone like Guy Kelton.

"Well," Guy hesitated for a long, thoughtful moment, "We could *kill* him!"

The idea sprang into his head after Patrick told him his whole story. It made Guy feel a boiling anger growing rapidly within, and that was obvious to Patrick. For a moment, Patrick was concerned about the killing because Guy had addressed it as a "we" act. They'd had a lengthy talk about what had happened. Patrick told Guy about his miseries, how he was now forced to work for a drug dealer, how he couldn't get out of it and how it was destroying his life. He wasn't sure why he had told Guy all that, but he felt it was okay to do so, that he could actually trust this man.

They didn't discuss it further. Patrick didn't want to seem like he didn't want it to happen, nor did he want to be clear about wanting it to happen. To Guy, it was all the same. Killing those innocent men and getting away with it had made him feel untouchable and invincible, that he would feel no remorse whatsoever killing a criminal, a lowlife like Barton. He wanted to see if by killing such a person he would be caught and punished for it or be left alone. He wanted to take it to the next level, to go to the extreme. To kill someone, who *deserves* to die, with intent.

He couldn't help but think about it. He could just go into this person's office and shoot him heartlessly, without blinking…three in the chest and perhaps an extra one in the head, just to make sure. His mind had been switched off, not taking in any sensibility. Maybe by doing so, by killing this Barton, his soul will be saved and his sanity would be half restored. But he had to retrieve his gun first. He left it somewhere in the apartment.

Tonight. It will have to happen tonight.

As for Patrick, the inimical thought only made him more insecure. Would he do it? Would that stranger kill this despicable man and save him and his Mandy? Why would he do that? Would that mean that he, Patrick, would be a conspirator in this murder? So many questions.

"It'd come to one thing in the end wouldn't it? Just one little silly thing. Now the tricky part is, you wouldn't know what that one thing is until the end actually arrives," he was speaking in a low voice, as if to himself, sitting on the chair at the table. Mandy was loitering around the apartment, trying to locate her women's magazine, dawdling, doing her best to act normal.

"So what are we supposed to do in between? Wait for the end? Worry and wait. Predict, speculate, think, wonder, expect, hope?" he added, again to himself.

A soft hand touched his shoulder.

"What are you talking about Patty?"

He looked up at her and then returned to staring blankly, hanging his head.

"Nothing you and I could do that would change anything. We could try but really, what's the point? The end would remain the same. And the 'one thing' would remain there too. Just waiting for us, to strike us hard in the face. To cripple us with the reality that we've always been trying to run away and hide from."

It seemed to Mandy that Patrick was blathering, he must be drunk, she thought to herself, but dared not to mention it. Not that she had seen him drunk many times.

"It will haunt us, and then it will eat us whole like a monster. We could hide behind our friends, we could run away with our lovers, we could lock ourselves away from the world, and it would still be there. Let's not kid ourselves. We could never win. The end will get us…in the end."

Mandy sat herself on the chair beside him, wrapped one arm around his shoulder, and held his hand with hers, slipping her fingers through his. Her eyes were filled with sadness. She, too, has reached her limitation. Patience is running out of her.

"I don't know, darling," she said, putting her head over his shoulder and sighing deeply, "I am as daunted as you are."

Her heart could sense imminent danger approaching, soon. Something charged with coagulated ugliness. And she was really worried about something else. She had never heard Patrick talk in such a detached manner before.

Patrick fell asleep moments later, sitting there on the chair, head on the table, supported by both his arms. When he woke up the place was dark and Mandy was gone, but where? He picked himself up, feeling a strong headache, yawning like a baby, his eyes he could barely keep open. He dragged himself up against the window, just to see the calm of the night dominating the streets.

Turning back to the table, Patrick's breath almost seized at the sight he saw. He saw *himself*, sitting there on the chair, and sleeping at the table. It was the only bright spot in the room.

Subconsciously, he backed up until his back touched the wall. His eyes were bulging and blinking crazily. His other self woke up and stood—just like *he* had a moment earlier—and now was coming towards him, to stare out the window. Patrick, stepping out of the other's way, felt his heartbeats quickening. Suddenly he felt hot and was petrified by the strange voices echoing in his ears. What these voices were saying he could not understand. The voices were distorted and disorganized.

Patrick's other self climbed onto the windowsill.

"No" said Patrick to himself quietly, "*NO!*" he yelled, stretching out his hand to stop himself from committing suicide, but he felt a burn of flame over his hand.

"Nooooooo!" But it was too late. For a few seconds there was just silence and blackness and a burning sensation on Patrick's hand, and then there was a massive rocking sound.

It was Mandy closing the door behind her, and Patrick was now awake, sweating and breathing like a man who'd just run a thousand miles. "It was just a dream", he told himself, "just a nightmare!"

"Honey, I brought us some ice-cream."

Just before arriving at his destination, Guy Kelton stopped at a hot-dog stand, thinking about what he was about to do. He stood, his hands in his pockets, staring at the Chinese man making hot-dogs. He looked up at the three-story redbrick building, just off Capital Avenue. He could see people emerging through the gate, most wearing heavy expressions, a few were smiling at each other and waving goodnight. It surprised him to see so many people working so late. It was almost seven now.

"What you want?" yelled the chubby, bawdy Chinese man to Guy and the latter answered with a simple headshake.

Guy couldn't understand why the Chinese man appeared to be looking at him in a suspicious manner. There was something about him that made Guy feel endangered, but most people looked at him that way. They all stared at him as if he was some kind of alien, or at least that's the impression he got. Just like that lady at the bookstore entrance; she'd gazed at him in complete astonishment as though she were staring at the reincarnated Jesus Christ or something.

Guy took a few steps away from the hot-dog stand and leaned his back on the nearest wall to him, not taking his eyes off the gate at Karmafoods, across the street. He felt the gun with his hand, tucked in the back of his pants.

The gun had been in the same place where he had hid it, under his bed pillow; he'd had no problems locating it, like he'd expected earlier, when he stopped by his apartment to pick it up for his mission, soon after his short meeting with Patrick, which was no less deviant than their previous encounter.

He could imagine how it would go; he would enter smoothly into Barton's office, without being noticed, after everyone else has gone. Patrick had told him that Barton stays behind to check the books. He would empty a couple of rounds into his victim—probably one in the chest and one in the head—instead of the four bullets he'd been thinking of earlier. He would go in and out in a flash.

That's the image he had in mind, but of course, he also knew that it could maybe happen unexpectedly differently. Things don't usually go according to plan, as he had learnt the hard way. Sometimes one can have such a perfect idea of how things would go that it distorts their perceptiveness to reality. But he's ready for it all. Now he has nothing to fear. It's all the same to him.

He sneaked silently through the corridors of the company's offices. A security guard stopped him and asked him what his business was.

"Got a special package for Mr. Barton," Guy was fast enough to answer.

"Right," said the guard and guided him to Barton's office.

A few minutes later he was on the third floor, outside Barton's office. He took a deep breath and barged in without thinking twice. There he was, sitting behind a large desk with a lot of money and papers scattered over it.

Barton stood up violently to protest but before he could say a word the gun was pointed at him. Guy surprised himself that he couldn't pull the trigger straight away. He looked at his victim's face, shocked and frightened. No one said a word. Both men could hear each other's breaths.

And then there was a click, and another. "It's jammed!" Guy cursed himself and his gun, and attempted to fix the situation quickly, but what did he know about guns?

"It's fucking jammed!" he said in disbelief.

Barton wasn't that quick to react but he did, eventually. He reached down to the desk cupboard and pulled out his own gun. It was a small revolver.

"Shit!" mumbled Guy, with a stunned face, covering himself with both his arms. At that moment he thought that was it. It was the moment of punishment. It was the moment God would take vengeance on him. He closed his eyes and waited for a few seconds, awaiting the bullet that would end his life. But nothing happened. Barton's gun was empty.

"Goddamit!' he yelled, remembering that he emptied the chambers of bullets when he was cleaning his piece the day before.

He searched for the bullets inside the cupboard as Guy slowly took away his protective arms and opened his eyes, realizing how stupid he was to think that this would have protected him from the bullets. Both men were busy in a crazy moment, each trying to fix their gun dilemma.

A heavy, sharp hit on the head awakened Guy from his useless attempts to work the gun. Something was thrown at him; it opened one of the old cuts he'd sustained in the car accident. He felt blood oozing out.

At his feet he saw Barton's revolver and raising his head, he found its owner picking the phone up to call for help, so he lunged like a wild horse towards him and jumped over the desk, which was not a smart move at all, because upon landing, he revived more of his earlier wounds and bruises. The pain was blinding.

Now everything was happening so fast it felt more like a dream to Guy than reality, like watching a film on fast-forward. He picked himself up and saw Barton making a getaway.

"Help!" he heard him scream "Help!"

Guy found a lighter in the shape of a fat short column, made of marble—almost the size of a baseball—and grabbed it with a fastball hold and threw it with all his might straight at the running man's back. He heard a loud awkward sound as the marble slapped flesh, and then a thud.

Strike!

Barton was on the floor. Guy approached with tentative steps, wondering what he should do. Barton lay on the floor moaning from the hit. Should he finish the job? *Could* he finish it? And how? With what? He looked around for something, the thought of just leaving everything and running away lurked but he shook it off instantly. He picked up the heavy lighter again. His adrenaline was pumping insanely,

Barton began moving and trying to stand. Guy offered him a hand to help him but as soon as he was on his feet, Guy landed the lighter with all his power to the side of Barton's head. The blow was fatal. He hit him with such force that blood splattered everywhere, on the floor, the walls, over him.

This time there was no moaning, no movement, no breathing.

Barton was dead. Guy was beginning to panic. He found it very difficult to breathe and struggled sucking in air, which was now saturated with the smell of a man's blood. But it was different, the smell of blood this time was different from before.

It took him a moment to calm himself down and get back to his senses, he was sweating and blood was running down his forehead. Realizing the capabilities of his malicious, destructive, murderous self both frightened and excited him. He walked with ease out of the office, hand holding the bloodied marble lighter, through the corridors, making his exit. Then he remembered the gun. He went back into the office, his heart racing.

The body was still there, unmoving. He scanned the whole place and then walked with heavy steps to the desk, knelt down and looked for the gun. It was lying behind the dustbin, and a stack of one-hundred-dollar bills sat there as well. He picked the gun and the money up and stood.

Guy flipped through the bills with his index finger; they were new bills, crisp and fresh. There were a few more stacks on the desk.

"Hell, why not?" he thought, grabbing a couple more, buried them into his pockets, slid the gun into the back of his pants and hurried himself out.

At the main gate the same security guard met him.

"Hey! You got sorted?" he asked, and just at that moment he saw the blood on Guy's hand.

The security guard froze, confused and taken aback. With a smooth voice Guy replied "yes," and passed right by the guard, who stood, helplessly, astonished, staring at the trail of blood left on the floor.

Chapter 25

It was getting way too much to take. Things had been deteriorating and it didn't seem that they would get any better any time soon. There was a lot of misery and depression here for her. Would there be more? Very likely. That's why she had to do something about it. She couldn't just sit there and wait for the next blow to strike. Last night she decided, there won't be a next blow. She will draw a line and she will cross that line. Cross over to the new, fresh side and leave the ugly, destructive side behind. And she will look ahead and walk on and on and on and never look back again. She will walk until the line cannot be seen anymore.

That's what Christina Heywood will do.

She couldn't understand why bad things kept happening to her. What did she ever do to deserve it all? She'd been a good girl all her life and now life was having a go at her, relentlessly. First it had been her father, many years ago, abandoning her. And now, and in the space of a couple of months, she'd lost her job, her mother and any chance of happiness with someone she loved and cared for. Anyone in a situation like this would have to consider that one unspeakable solution. The one which at that particular time, seemed to be the only way out.

Yes, Christina did think about killing herself. She thought of bringing an end to her miserable life, by slashing her wrist, throwing herself off a building, maybe the Doyen Tower, or taking all the pills she can lay her hands on. But she knew that even if she really wanted to do it, she could not. Not that it was the first time she'd thought about it. There comes a time for almost everybody, when they contemplate their suicide. Contemplate how to do it and how it will affect those around them, sometimes it helps not having anyone anymore—like in Christina's case now, contemplate the feelings and thoughts you'd go through just before you do it.

Everything, everyone, is gone: Her father, her mother, her lover…and even her friend. Mandy! Where is Mandy now? Oh well, Christina told herself, nothing matters anymore.

That's what life always does to you, drives you to the edge. It's up to you to then decide whether to throw yourself off, or hang in there until some kind of miracle comes and pulls you back to safety. The thing is, if neither of these two things happens and you are stuck in between, chances are you're going to lose your mind. Go insane.

Aaron's funeral was a crowded one, compared to her mother's. Some suited young men stood about behind a line of family and relatives, all looking sad, and anxious to leave the place. Nobody liked funerals.

It was a Sunday, a quiet day. She almost didn't go; when she woke up that morning she knew she couldn't, or didn't want to, go through another funeral, she felt numb. She went through the motions with automatic notion. She wore a black skirt and charcoal grey top, with a black waist-length jacket.

Again, just like the day of her mother's funeral, the dark clouds gathered and hung over the cemetery. But it didn't rain.

There was an elderly couple, who must have been Aaron's parents, who kept glancing at Christina with unwelcoming eyes, which made her feel like she had no right to be there. Their eyes were full of blame and anger. Even his sister, Maryana, scorned her. Little baby Suzana would never be held in her uncle's arms again.

Christina has never spoken to any of them, and she wasn't about to do so at the funeral. So she left before the casket was even lowered and said her last goodbye in her heart.

When she got back home, she locked herself in the bathroom and broke down. Maybe it was a bit selfish, but she kept thinking of herself and how she was going to overcome of all these overwhelming experiences. She was crying, mourning the death of her own spirit. She conceived three stabs in the heart in a row. Three magnificent blows, each greater pain than the one before. She felt her own blood seeping out of her broken heart as she cried

Now she's thinking of leaving entirely, leaving for good, out of this place, this house, this town, this domicile for sorrow and pain and neglect and sadness, with the slim hope of forgetting all that had happened to her. What she would do to wipe it all from her mind? To have a clean and subtle mind, like a piano song, what she would do to just have that face erased from her memory? That face. The stranger's face, the face of the man who came in her dream and took away her lover, who she almost bumped into near the book store, and who she remembers seeing some place before.

Christina recalled the incident at her mother's funeral, wherein a man appeared out of nowhere and approached them. The lone stranger. She never paid much heed to him then, even though it was a very suspicious and bizarre incident. That man, as she remembers now, spoke with Mandy's boyfriend. Could he be the one? But what would he have wanted with Patrick? Perhaps she should ask him, ask Patrick. Try and find out more about the stranger. Maybe she would find an answer to all the questions she has been asking herself.

Was it the same man? Was it the one who murdered her Aaron? As much as she wanted to leave it all behind and turn her back on that chapter of her life, she couldn't. If her doubts were true then she wouldn't be able to live with herself without doing something.

And at that moment there was only one thing she could do.

Chapter 26

▼

John Pinkerton thought about it hard. What should he do? Well, he would have to tell the police eventually. He knew that the picture of the smashed car he'd just seen in the paper was the murderer's car. But wouldn't the police figure that out already by themselves? He had given them the description of the car.

The little piece accompanying the picture, written by someone called James Akron, said that the driver of the car was taken to hospital but was not identified. A young couple driving back home from a party found him unconscious on the road and called an ambulance. At the hospital he had been treated for his wounds and injuries, which were not serious. He then, strangely, disappeared without trace. Hospital staff couldn't get any information about him. "He's probably just another car thief", a hospital doctor was quoted in the paper.

Mr. Pinkerton, so far, had not told anyone about what he knew. Not even his wife. Well, in the state she was still in, she would probably never get it anyway. Actually, it might have made things worse if he did tell her. So he'd shut his mouth for the time being and begun thinking about a way to make the most out of this entire bizarre situation.

Suddenly he began asking himself all sorts of questions—something he's not used to do, usually if he had a question he would ask his wife, not himself—"Where did that man go? Was the car really stolen? Why don't the police investigate more in the case? Could it be that they got the wrong man?"

It was all mixed up and didn't make any sense. But Mr. Pinkerton, for his own reasons, *wanted* to make sense out of it. So he sat down in his cranky oak chair, at his oak desk, in the basement of the house he and his wife had shared for the past fifteen years, to mull it over.

John seldom goes down the basement. Not because he doesn't want to but because his wife doesn't like him to do so. Today was one of those days that he had to be there.

He sat on his oak chair and he wrote.

He wrote down notes and points in a blue notebook, trying to draw up a scheme, a plan, to achieve his goal. Suddenly, it began to become clearer to him. What he wanted to do. Now was the chance to do it. This was the opportunity that he must not let go by.

He remembered his grandfather's saying, "Don't underestimate what you got, no matter how trivial it may seem to everyone". And John wasn't about to underestimate what he knew now. What he knew was that he was the only one who saw the murderer leave the store and get into the car, that same car which was in the papers. What he knew was that the man who was in hospital was the murderer and not just a car thief, and that his wife had actually seen him. She was the only one that could identify him. More importantly and vitally, he knew now that the police have got the wrong man.

But John wasn't interested in bringing the right man to justice—he wasn't a hero and he didn't want to be one. He was not about to do what he was about to do for the well-being of mankind. That's not really one of the virtues of the people of Okay, nor a matter of their interest. All that John was interested in was getting that money.

Of course, there had been no such thing as $10,000 that the murderer stole from the Pinkerton's mini-market, although John had insisted there was. He wasn't sure why he'd said that in the first place. Why he'd lied. It was hard to buy, and the police weren't about to believe it when he told them. It was an automated reflex. He hadn't thought about it twice. It'd just come out of his mouth.

"Our $10,000 is missing," he'd kept telling them "That murdering son-uva-bitch took it," a tremble of uncertainty in his voice "All of it!"

A few minutes after he'd said it, he'd regretted it and cursed himself, silently, for his stupidity for trying to pull such a stunt—not that he'd not been a sleazy bastard before but this was way out of line. The police hadn't seemed to be bothered much about it, despite the fact that they pretty much knew he was lying to them. Which puzzled John and drove him further, wanting to see the end of it.

The plan was beginning to unveil for him. It was getting clearer and now seeming more likely to work than when he'd first thought about it. Once he had his hands on the money, he'd be out of here. He'd run away, away from this rotten place, away from his bed-bound wife. It would be tough to leave her behind after all these years, after all they had shared, but it must be done. And he was convinced that she would forgive him, she would understand why he would do such a thing.

He would start all over. With someone new. Maybe it's not too late after all. Being forty-five years old doesn't mean it's too late for a new start, does it?

No.

That same night, Guy Kelton, needing time to think, was taking a walk in the calm and deserted streets. Clouds were, curiously, gathering, forming a fluffy, wavy sheet of grey across the black night sky. Through one hole between the patches of cloud, Guy could see the moon. Strangely full and perfect and blinding bright. But he could see it only for a moment, as the grey clouds moved across, filling that gap in-between. "Is it going to rain?" Guy asked himself.

"Are you going to rain?" he said, as he looked up at the sky, "Well, that would be a bit too freaky, wouldn't you think?"

A passing car brought him back to his senses. "Great", he thought, "now I'm talking to the sky! Next thing I'll know is the sky talking back to me". And at that thought he stopped walking and kept staring blankly at nothing, just anticipating the sky to speak.

But it didn't.

"I'm going nuts." Maybe he's not. But one thing he is for sure is a murderer. He has killed three people. He was surprised how calm he was, having just killed another man not more than a couple of hours ago. After he'd left the Karmafoods building he'd begun walking aimlessly, casually, as if nothing had happened at all.

There was a small water fountain on the side of the pavement, which was in the shape of a naked little boy peeing. Guy stared at the stone-boy's eyes. They scared him. He then stared at the statue's penis and found that there was a missing testicle. He looked both sides and almost laughed out loud, the boy had only one huge, almost flat, testicle. Seemed that the sculptor was a little bit too confused about how to go around it, or maybe he'd just been having a laugh!

He smiled at it and dipped both his hands into the water. It was cold, sending shivers through his chest. He washed off the blood from his face and as he did so the image came back to him. It re-played in the back of his head slowly, seeing how the wound was caused, how the blood spurted out of it in chunks and splatters.

Guy threw up.

The numbness he'd been feeling had surpassed his wildest imagination. It had crippled his mind and clouded his feelings, turning him into a murdering zombie. Everything was as far from real as those dreams he'd been having.

Those dreams? He tried to remember all of them, to remember the details. But it'd been hard for him lately. He knows they are there in his head somewhere. Why can't he remember them? But then again, why should he? One thing he remembered distinctly is the gate. That huge black gate he suddenly found himself in front of while walking to work that morning. He wanted to go through it. Go beyond it. Why couldn't he? Something had stopped him! Suddenly, an overwhelming desire to know took hold of him. He wanted so bad to see what was on the other side. He must know. Perhaps, as crazy as all what'd been happening to him seemed, perhaps once he did that, it would make sense of everything. Perhaps he would find the answers there.

So he made up his mind that tomorrow morning he would walk that exact same path, at that exact same time, and do and think exactly as he did that day, and keep hoping that the world will lose sense of reality once more and he will find the gate.

When he got near to his apartment building—safely, without any bizarre incidents or random acts of violence—it was almost midnight. But of course he didn't know that. He didn't even know that he'd spent the last five hours roaming the town.

At one point, he'd sat on a wooden bench at the side of the Town's Park for two hours, just trying so hard to block his thoughts, freeze his mind. He'd sat there and stared down at a leaf on the ground. Vibrating from the gentle wind, sometimes moving a slight nod left or right. He'd found himself not thinking about anything but that leaf. Where it came from, which tree it belonged to, what was it doing here? He'd wished he could ask it and he'd wished it would talk to him, but then he'd thought maybe he should be more careful what he wishes for, because lately all sorts of unthinkable things had been happening: A gray pigeon with black and white feathered-wings had flown just above his head, the flapping of its wings echoing. He'd looked up at it and watched it as it crossed from one tree to the next and then the next and the next, till it couldn't be seen anymore.

It was then, for some reason, it had occurred to him that there was always someone who could easily identify him for the murders he had committed. There were witnesses to each one of his three crimes, who had had a good look at him. There were the few men in the bar when he shot the fat bartender, there was the old lady at the mini-market when he shot the well-dressed young handsome man, there was the security guard, who even though he didn't actually see Guy doing it, could identify him as the man who came in clean and walked out with blood stains over him, leaving a dead Barton with a smashed head behind.

They had all seen him. Seen his face. Stared at him in awe and bewilderment and shock. They had all seen what he did, and could easily be the reason for him getting what he deserved; being put behind bars, for the rest of his life, or maybe worse. Yet, until this day and this moment, he was a free man, walking freely among the casual masses, just your ordinary Okay citizen. Perhaps for not much longer. Perhaps the cavalry were on their way to get him.

Guy, in an attempt to make sense of it, put his current freedom down to having one of those forgettable faces, the type that you can't remember just minutes after you've seen it. His face and his expressions were dull. Nothing special. Nothing that makes him standout, even if he were a wolf in a flock of sheep, he would still be unrecognizable. Or maybe it could be that the people of Okay, just don't give a damn about a thing? All they want is to stay out of trouble, keep out of sight, avoid the headlights, and lurk in the dull mundane shadows of life. What sort of a person would you be if you witnessed a crime and you knew you could do something about it that could make a good difference, but sit back tight and pretend that you have been blind? What sort of person would that make you?

Just a human being, that's what.

When he arrived home he found that Mr. Pickles wasn't around. Guy didn't see him at the entrance of the building. That's how he knew the time. Pickles shuts the gate and locks up at midnight every night. Whoever comes later has to use the back door to enter. A key to the door is kept in a little sachet, in the plant-tray, over the high, small boxed window ledge; they are supposed to step over the box, reach over to the plant, pull the sachet out, open the door with the key and then return it to the same place and lock the door again from the inside.

So Guy did that. And as usual the building welcomed him with its ever-so quietness and lifelessness. He climbed the stairs with boredom, keeping his head down, looking at his feet going up one step at a time, with a gentle thud. He wondered if the doorman would hear his steps, or the other tenants of this gloomy building, as the thudding became rhythmic, echoing lightly up and down the stairway.

When he got to Mrs. Jacker's apartment he stopped momentarily at the door, very thoughtful. He then remembered the stash of money he'd taken from Barton's office. He pulled it out of his trousers and placed it right against the widow's door and then was on his way again.

As he got closer to his apartment, climbing up the last set of steps, with his head still staring at his feet, he began to feel woozy; a moment of sleepiness that made his head lighter. He felt strange, a sudden change. He knew that feeling; he'd felt it before. But right now he couldn't remember anything—not even his own name. He was suddenly finding it hard to focus and concentrate, to think of things, and everything around him and inside of him seemed to slow down.

He took another step, but this time there was no thud.

A blink.

He was standing alone in that same dark alley again, with the tall stretching walls on both sides. Even though he couldn't seen anyone around, Guy felt there was another presence, another entity, with him, around him, near him—spirits, or ghosts, or thoughts? They tried to talk to him, maybe warn him not to go forward. But their warnings went unheard, unrecognized; if anything those warnings only drove his curiosity further to see what this place held for him.

He was going through the same motions again. His mind struggled what to make of this place, he was almost certain he had been there before. But at that moment he wasn't even thinking of that. It was like when you visit a place in your dreams that you only realize you have been to, or seen before, after you wake up.

The sky was getting grayer with black clouds dotted about and there was a vacuous feeling to the place that deprived it of any sense of life or reality.

The gate stood proudly tall. Intimidating and profound, it challenged Guy, or so he felt. Daring him to touch it, to try and go through it. For a long moment, that seemed to last a lifetime—during which a fatherless child was born to a weakened woman. He grew to become a young man who sparkled in school and shined in college, and who made a man of himself, and lived a life full of trivial events that he forgot the minute he had them. And had special moments that became the core of his sweet memories that lasted his whole lifetime. The man grew older and older, after a marriage that he had foreseen in a dream he had on a long, quiet summer night, to a good looking woman working at the candy store across the street to his house, which he had inherited from a grandfather he had never known or met.

Then he got old and then he died. And a whole lifetime was gone—Guy stood, gaping at the gate, with a desire so strong to see what was behind it.

There was no old man this time.

Just a piercing silence that numbed the mind and killed the heart, there was no air to breath between the tall walls either side of this place. He finally stretched his hand out, ever so slowly, feeling every fraction of a second passing by, every movement.

His hand touched the surface of the gate, hot and cold at the same time, and began a lengthy grind of pushing it open. As he pushed further and harder with his hand, he felt little sharp teeth jutting out of its metallic surface and cutting through his palm's skin.

Then in a quick loop, it was open. And there was a bright light that could have blinded the whole of mankind. Then, bit-by-bit, things began to show.

And Guy Kelton saw things no other living man had ever seen and things that no other man will ever see.

Chapter 27

▼

He sat on the sofa, alone. To his right sat GoGo, on the chair. The big bald man stood in front of Guy, just about two meters away. The third man stood to the left and was leaning lazily on the wall.

"Now, boy. Tell me," began the ugly mobster "Where is Patty?"

They'd appeared out of the shadows as soon as he'd entered his place. It was dark and he was so dizzied and numbed and confused to realize he needed light to see his way around. He'd just come from a long walk, after murdering a man he knew little about apart from being a 'bad' man, and that was based on the opinion of just one individual who he, Guy, didn't know that closely anyway, and to top all of that, he'd seen things. One of those dreams, visions, he'd been having, and that has jammed his mind temporarily.

"Who?" he said.

He had been trying to recollect what he'd seen, placing one hand over his head and the other stretched out to make his path to bed, when he bumped into something big, which Guy was certain wasn't a piece of furniture! It was too meaty to be a closet. He heard heavy breathing, and with his hand felt a big chest heaving, and then a push. Whoever it was standing there in the dark, in the middle of his dingy little apartment, had pushed him down to the sofa, where he felt something round and hard under his bum. And then a light was switched on, and the three figures had emerged.

In the first moment, Guy had thought maybe they were cops—it was possible that the building guard had managed to make a quick identification. Hell, there could have been cameras even, he never thought of that before—but the look on their faces, the smell, their aura…and of course…GoGo, his good ole school buddy! He remembered that face pretty well, even after all these years. And it slowly came back to him, all the crimes and horrors and violations GoGo committed even as a little kid, as a teenager, and all the stories he'd heard about him.

"You know, I liked you," said GoGo, "Back at school, you seemed like a nice guy and I wanted you to be on my side. Boy, this town sure is a small one. And it looks I was right, boys. The sonuvabitch killed our man," he said, turning to his mates.

Guy knew he was in trouble now, big trouble, and although he couldn't deny that he felt fear within him, he was surprisingly cool and calm, considering all he'd been going through, done and seen. His head was unclear, thoughts and memories and ideas all scrambled together trying to find a place of their own.

There were flashes from what he'd seen as he was just climbing the stairs to his apartment—a collection of magnified horrors, dreams and nightmares, shattered and broken and evil, horrifying crimes and all sorts of things that make the skin crawl—making it harder for him to focus on the situation in hand.

There was also a vision.

"Look man, I ain't gonna do the I'm-not-gonna-ask-you-again, gonna-torture-you-and-cut-your-fingers shit. They only do that in movies. In the end it's your life. You don't answer the fuckin' question, you simply die."

A nod at the big man resulted in the latter producing a big gun. A Desert Eagle, reckoned Guy. Guy knew deep inside that he would soon die, on this very sofa, in this shithole of an apartment. He had it coming; he knew that would be the only end for him. Maybe he should fight for it, do something. Think fast. Stall. Why though? Why would he? There isn't much left to live for anyway.

"Patty who?" he pleaded.

"Your friend Patrick," said GoGo, "There's a score to be settled with you two. The Big Boss is pretty mad, Guy. And that ain't good for nobody,"

"Well," began Guy, still trying to figure out a way to get out of this dead-end situation "you are going to kill me even if I tell you. Not that I know. But let's say if I told you about one place, you would still kill me, am I right?" His heart was pounding. GoGo pulled a smirk that said, "Yes".

"I thought so." Guy said. What else? Keep talking. "Ok. You can kill me, but please don't hurt Biscuit. I don't want him to see me dead."

A long pause and three puzzled faces.

"*Who?*" The big man with the big gun asked.

"My kitten. Biscuit. Please don't hurt him,"

GoGo broke into laughter. The third man was still leaning on the wall, shaking his head. This was it. The only chance to do whatever it was Guy should try and do was now.

Quick as a bee he jumped backwards and knelt behind the sofa.

"What the hell?" someone yelled. Guy heard fast footsteps. GoGo stood up and pulled his gun. But before he pointed it at the frightened and panicked Guy, a flying object came rushing at him. He covered his face with his free arm. Crash. A loud crack echoed in the room. It was broken. The object was none other than a baseball thrown by Guy with full strength. His favorite one. It was another satisfying pitch, just as deadly as the one he threw at Barton. The ball had been there under his butt on the sofa.

"Kill him. *Now!*" boomed GoGo, in apparent agony.

The third man fired the first shot at the same time Guy was leaping over the sofa. The bullet hit the ground. Another shot was heard—this time from the big man—it sank into the sofa, producing a muffled sound and some shreds of flying sponge!

Now Guy was standing up. He was in the center of the room. Behind him was GoGo, still struggling with the pain of his broken arm. In front of him stood the human wall. Guy dropped to the ground in the fraction of a second it took GoGo and the Big Man to fire.

Guy looked up. He was miraculously not hurt. A quick glance at GoGo brought relief, the intimidating mobster laid on the chair unmoving. Dead? Looked like it.

The big man was struggling to keep his balance. Guy knew he was also hit, but where exactly he couldn't tell. That man was so big that a little bullet hole wouldn't be visible to the regular human eye.

Run.

Guy, with full thrust, ran toward the flailing thug. The third man pointed his gun at Guy and fired another shot. He missed. Guy jumped at Big Man, and heard a third shot. Guy was now hanging to the big man's meaty neck. He turned and fell over him. A fourth shot by the third man sank into the fat of the big man's ass!

Guy could barley breathe. He felt his ribs cracking under the weight. He thought he would be crushed to death. Three long seconds later he felt the final breath of Big Man against his face, it smelled of mint.

The third thug was now just a step and a half away. Guy reached for the gun and managed to pull it free from the big man's enormous hand. He held his breath. The third man, swearing and cursing, tried to push his colleague aside, a task that wasn't easy.

As he kept trying, Guy realized he had to do something very soon. But it was very difficult to aim at something when a dead man's face is staring right back at you and his massive weight is crushing your chest.

So he just raised the gun up a notch and fired one crazy shot to the ceiling in the hope of scaring the man off. The next he heard was a thud. Slowly, he began to open his eyes, first the right one, and with that he saw the body of the third man dead on the floor, blood splattered against the top of the wall and on the ceiling. The crazy shot hit the bastard right under his jaw and went through his head.

Then, hesitantly, Guy opened his left eye and with that he saw GoGo standing with his gun in his hand. He placed his broken arm by his left hip.

There was a short tense moment.

In one move both men aimed at each other and started pulling the trigger. It was loud. The whole apartment was alive with echoing sounds of bullets.

Lights flickered.

There were two different sounds: Bang! Boof! Bang! Boof! Bang! Boof! Bang! Boof! Boof! Bang! Bang! Bang! Tick! Tick! Tick! Empty magazine. Guy fired all the shots. His ears hurt. The sound of the shots rang like they had bells of Doom in them. For a moment he did not feel anything. He was not sure if he was hit or not. His vision was unclear and blurry from the gunpowder and smoke.

Slowly, he began to feel his hand holding the gun vibrating, his finger touching the trigger, tapping on it, mechanically.

Can't breath, can't breathe! Need air.

He moved himself from underneath the pile of fat and flesh that laid upon him, with all the strength that was left in him. It took a while but he managed to do it. It was wet. The body was seeping blood and it wetted Guy's clothes. He felt some of the thick liquid over his face.

For a few minutes, Big Man was like the death angel himself, holding Guy's breaths and making gasps for the last ones as he prepared to reach in for his victims' soul to take it. But Guy was still alive only thanks to him—or his fat. He'd received all of GoGo's random bullets. His flesh had taken the impact of the bullets and they seemed to have all settled within it. Guy knew how lucky he was, if it had been a thinner man, like the third thug over there, the bullets would have gone through and into Guy.

A look at GoGo was not sheer pleasure. Yes, finally he was dead, but the poor guy had holes—big ones—in him everywhere: Head, chest, stomach, legs, arms, everywhere. His body swam in a pool of its own blood. It was a mess. The whole place had turned red; blood on the walls, floor, and furniture, everywhere. The smell of blood—which Guy was already getting used to—intoxicated the room.

A sticky, soft, wet object was dangling on Guy's neck. He reached for it and picked it. It looked like a nutshell. It was bloody and mushy. Guy turned to the massive blob of flesh in astonishment and disgust.

The piece in his hand was part of Big Man's brains.

Chapter 28

He was sweating when he woke up in the morning. It must have been some dream, he thought to himself, brushing the dirty white sheet aside. His mind was kicking in very slowly. There was the thought about getting up and ready for work at first, but that was shook off immediately, remembering that he'd stopped going to work, that he'd been jobless for quite some time now. That one thought triggered a series of memories, of everything that had happened to him over the past few days and weeks, up to last night.

His ability to think broke down. His heart tried desperately to convince him that it was just another dream; that it did not actually happen. But his mind knew better.

He sat up on the bed and looked out the window; the sun was still making its way up. The room was still a grey place. Guy wiped his sweaty forehead with his forearm and ran his palm over his face, neck and chest gently, resting it over his heart, feeling its heavy beats. He was scared, if all that his mind told him were true, there would be three bodies scattered across his dingy apartment. But again, he told himself that it couldn't have been real because if it were, then there would have been cops all over the place, right? There would have to be. Because there had been a lot of shooting, someone must have heard; someone—Pickles if not anyone else—would have called the police. And if it was all true then how on earth did he end up in bed, in his shorts, and sleeping soundly through the night?

He kept staring out the window, waiting for the sun, which was now coming into view, its light and rays spreading around and reaching into his apartment through the smudged glass window. He closed his eyes and kept them shut for what he felt was a long moment then he turned his head to the right, towards the center of the apartment, where the few pieces of furniture rested. Guy was afraid. A part of him didn't want to look in case his eyes came upon three dead bodies splayed across the floor, but another part of him compelled his eyes to open, slowly, to know for certain. He kept telling himself that it *must* have been a dream. There won't be anything or anyone. The place will be tidy.

And there wasn't. And it was.

A great sense of relief washed over him. He remembered to breath. Guy threw his feet to the floor and pushed himself up and off the bed. Only then did he feel the blinding headache hitting him. It hit him so hard he almost dropped down to the ground in an instant, but somehow he stayed standing, feeling woozy.

Five minutes later he was dressed and ready to leave. He inspected the place one more time, but no proof of what had happened last night was visible. No blood stains splattered against the walls, no bullet shells, nothing. As much as his mind was convinced that it was a dream, his heart was still at unease, unable to take sides between reality and fiction. It was a question of willpower, a true battle, and a raging war in which, like every other war, there is no wrong or right. But in which the most imposing and effective, at that certain time, would become the victor.

Guy walked out of his meek domicile reluctantly, fearing what the world would hold for him today, fearing what he'd proven he was capable of doing. As much as he preferred to stay in the safety of his bed all day long, he couldn't resist doing something. He decided he would go out and let whatever was going to happen, happen. This plan had proven to work so far, for better or worse of course is a matter of opinion, though nothing that had happened to him so far could be described as anything less than disastrous.

He started his journey down the stairs, a hand on the sidebar, the other wiping the sweat off his forehead. How could it be so hot? A few steps later and he froze still. The whole building was still and quiet.

He remembered the gate and the things he had seen.

She stayed up all night, she couldn't sleep, her mind busy coming up with different scenarios and conclusions, most of which were very disturbing, involving a lot of pain and death and hurt and destruction. She lay in bed staring at the ceiling hour after hour, breaking into tears whenever memories of her late mother or lover surfaced. She would doze off for a few minutes and then wake up again, going through the same ritual all over again.

At the break of dawn she had had enough and decided to go on with her plan, which wasn't much of a real plan anyway. All she knew that she had to do was go and find Patrick, Mandy's boyfriend, and try to get as much from him as she could about the strange fellow who she believed was Aaron's murderer. She had seen his face three times now, first at her mother's funeral, second when he came in her dream the day Aaron was killed, and once at the book store entrance on Park Avenue. She had to know about him: who was he? What's his connection with Patrick, if there was any? And the big one: was he really Aaron's murderer?

She got dressed and walked out of her miserable, lonesome house with haste. Within an hour she was standing in front of the door of Patrick Roymint's apartment. It was almost seven according to her wristwatch. She had a moment of hesitation and regret at coming here before knocking on the door. Knock-knock. Nothing, no answer. Another knock. And another. Still no answer. She stood anxiously, shuffling her foot. Then she heard movement.

"Who is it?" yelled a voice from behind the door.

"Open up."

The door was pulled open just a notch and when Patrick saw the unexpected visitor, he flung the door wide open in surprise.

"You!" he managed to say.

"Yes, me. We need to talk."

Patrick's head was swirling; he himself hadn't had any sleep the night before. His worries about what was going to happen were eating him alive. But the very second he saw *her*, all of that was swept away. His heart began to pound.

Christina gave him an awkward look. He was scruffy and ill-looking.

"Are you ok?" she asked. "Where is Mandy?"

"She's gone. She left," he said, not meeting her eyes. "Come in, please."

The place was a mess; it was obvious that someone had a rough night. Or even a rampage. Things were thrown everywhere, clothes and litter and broken things.

"What happened?"

"Oh, it doesn't matter now. It's all over," his voice was bitter and weak. "But you're here!"

"Yes," she said. "Yes I am." A stilted moment followed. Both remembered their first encounter at the park. Patrick couldn't stop thinking about this beautiful woman standing perkily in the center of his filthy apartment. She came for him, he was certain. "She loves me", he told himself.

"It's not what you think." she said, interrupting his sweet, silly thoughts. "I'm here because I have questions, and I am hoping you would help me find some answers. You don't have to, but I'm asking you anyway."

"Questions? What questions?" he quizzed. Now he was getting a bit nervous. Did she know about their plan? Did she somehow learn of what he had done?

"Questions about what?"

She told him everything, about the funeral, the dream, that face. She told him all about it, she didn't have anything to lose. It only dawned at her then that Patrick might be *his* partner, and that he wouldn't give him away even if he knew anything about what truly happened. For a second she thought about forgetting about it and running off out of that place. But she didn't. She had to trust him.

Patrick sat down as he listened, lips parted and red eyes widened. But he was not afraid anymore; the fragility of Christina had softened his worries and strengthened his heart. Her watery eyes were gorgeously compelling. He felt himself wanting to be exposed to her, so he went on and told her everything about his part in everything. He told her about the job and the drugs and the dreams and the gangs. He told Christina how he'd met Guy, although he couldn't give a sensible explanation about how they came to know each other, nor could he explain why he had felt there was some sort of bizarre connection between them. As for the mess in the apartment, he could only come up with the assumption that Mandy had left him and disappeared. She had probably had a mad fit the night before. He didn't find a note; she probably didn't leave one. He'd come back very late, and she was gone. What he didn't know was that GoGo and his gang has actually come to look for him before visiting Guy, and when they didn't find anyone around they'd trashed the place and left.

"Oh God!" whispered Christina softly, after along moment of silence. "We have to find him!" she urged Patrick, who looked down in shame for letting Christina down, for not knowing where to find Guy. "Sorry."

Christina hovered around the place, wondering what was going to happen next and what was she going to do. There was no logic to any of this. It was just madness. She decided to leave. She sighed and headed to the door, more hopeless and miserable then when she first came in through it.

"Wait!" jumped Patrick, remembering something. "I think I know where he might be."

Chapter 29

▼

As they drove in the Karmafoods van along the lonesome, empty road to Blossomville, the picture became clearer to Christina. Patrick explained more to her about the company's illegal operation, and how Mandy had known about it for a long time, how she'd been living in fear but never for a second showing it, even in the slightest, to anyone around her, not even her closest companion, himself.

They'd had a big argument over it the night before. They never usually had arguments. As far as he could remember, they'd never had one since they got together. Mandy had been upset and confused and very rattled. She'd decided that they could both simply just run away, go live with their aunt in the South, leaving everything behind and starting a new life altogether. He'd refused, saying that he couldn't leave now, for reasons mysterious and dark to him still.

Patrick turned to look at Christina, as they neared Jo & Jo's Store. There she was, he thought to himself, sitting right beside him. This gorgeous, subtle woman who had been stricken by grief from every angle, but who somehow still seemed to have the energy to go on. He wished he had the same willpower, the same strength, to be able to get Mandy and himself out of this mess. There was no point now. Mandy was gone.

"I'm sorry about your…"

"Don't." she interrupted. She was looking out the window, her head leaning against the cool glass. It was the first time she'd been through this street since the murder. She could still hear the music, feel the breeze, remembering every detail of the night before. As they drove by the store, she dared herself to look at it. When she did, she felt the sharp pain in her heart again, like a hard punch right into the exposed, fragile thing. Her eyes welled up, lips quivered. She looked away again, without saying a word, placing her head back against the window.

Patrick felt awkward. He was clumsy, certainly not the type who was good at providing comfort and consolation. Crying women always made him nervous, more so a woman as gorgeous as Christina. He would grow extremely agitated and flustered at the sight of a woman in tears; even as a little kid, every time his mother or sister started crying for some reason or the other he'd felt like that. That's why Mandy never cried in front of him and kept a straight, smiling face when she was around him. Patrick couldn't see how she managed it. He just realized that perhaps he'd been too selfish in their relationship. Perhaps he didn't want to be in it in the first place. Either way, he decided, Mandy did not deserve him.

"I found him in the bathtub, my father," Patrick began, his distant eyes staring ahead. "He drowned himself. Can you believe it? I have no idea how he did it. It must have taken some real strength. They had quite a hard time pulling his hands off the side handles; he gripped them with all his might," he explained, reliving the horrible moment in his head. "I came back one afternoon from school, straight into the bathroom. Just as I was standing there, unzipping my pants, I saw the water, on the floor. I pulled the curtains and there he was. Dead. Drowned. Just like my mother, just like my sister," he paused then, feeling his eyes sting with sudden warmth, thinking about Karla. She would've been 32 by now. Probably married, with kids. Christina sat up straight and looked at him with sad eyes. She wanted to say something but she was lost for words.

"That's awful," she eventually said "Mandy never mentioned anything…"

"I never told her."

"How old were you?"

"Doesn't matter, does it? What matters is that I know how it feels to lose people that you love, right in front of your eyes, to lose everything, everyone. It's not a pleasant thing. Not one bit. You become detached from your emotions, you grow numb, thick-skinned, indifferent, unimposing. You become redundant. You find it harder to care, to love. You give up. And you leave it on auto-drive. Just go with the flow. Your whole life becomes like the infinite space, empty, dark and endless."

Christina found herself reaching a hand to him, gently placing hers on his. She felt closer to him now, realizing what they had in common. They understood each other.

"That day, in the park, when we first met, remember?"

"Yes."

"What were you going to say then? Why did you come up to me? You didn't know who I was."

"I didn't. It was very strange, I just couldn't resist. I just had to speak to you, I don't know why or for what. But you looked very familiar. Like, you know, when you think you've seen someone in a dream? And then you see them in real life and you feel like there's a connection? Like you know them?"

"Yes," replied Christina, somberly "I do."

Just then, Patrick had another crazy revelation, which, just like most of the events of the last several weeks, did not make any sense. But he knew he had to do it. It came to him in a flash, a rush of an idea. Even though not knowing exactly what it was, he braked and turned the van violently around, and headed back towards Jo & Jo's Store.

"What the hell are you doing?!"

"I'm not sure," he said, "I think I know!"

The town seemed very restless but very tired. He walked hurriedly and with purpose, he had made up his mind and he wouldn't be backing out. He'd had enough.

He couldn't help but notice that the doorman still wasn't around, which was weird, as he was usually almost *always* guarding the gate at that time of the day. But Guy was relieved that he didn't see him. He didn't want any distractions. He didn't want to think about the things that had happened or the things that might have happened.

He was just going to walk into the Police station and hand himself in.

Dodging through the small crowds of people on the pavement and crossing the half-empty streets, Guy realized what a mad place this was. Full of empty people, aimless and purposeless. So much wrong ignored, so much evil endured. Is it the way of the world, of nature? Or is it the way of men? Perhaps what he was about to do was something that could make this place a better place. Perhaps, he thought, it would bring a sense of relief, some sort of peace, a kind of equilibrium. Hell, maybe even justice.

At the far corner at the bottom of the street, Guy saw a little girl standing alone, wearing a pretty little white dress, her golden, curly hair glowing. She looked like an angel, amidst all the darkness of the crowds. She was staring right back at him. She had a harmonica in her hand. It was Angela, the girl he'd met at the market, he remembered. He wanted to go up to her to say hello, maybe even play another tune for her, but he knew he had to focus on his task. Guy simply smiled and waved at her. Angela waved back, a sad look on her face. Then she disappeared.

He continued his walk to the station, keeping his eyes on the ground all the way, just like he always did. The Police station was situated between an old Church house and a boxing gym. It was a small building, one of the oldest in town. It used to be Okay's clinic for the insane, but due to a lack of patients and funding, it had been shut down and turned into a police building many years ago.

Guy couldn't help a muffled shriek at the horrible stink as he walked in to the reception area. A bald, fat officer sat behind the desk, munching a jam doughnut.

"Hello. I'm a murderer. I've killed many men. I'm here to give myself in,"

The officer just looked at him with a frown. He dismissed him with a hand gesture and resumed consuming his doughnut, getting the jam stuffing all over his face.

"I said I have committed murder—more than one actually. I want to make a confession."

"Church is next door."

"Look officer. I am a *murderer*. Get it?" Guy was finding it harder than he had first thought it would be. He was getting rather anxious. "Get the Sheriff. Do something, please," he pleaded. "I want to go to jail!" he shouted, punching the desk, just as Sheriff Markovic walked in.

"What the fuck is going on here? Who the hell are you?"

"My name is Guy Kelton. I have murdered seven innocent men," he said, and then corrected, "Well, actually, only two of them were innocent."

"What the hell are you talking about, pig-face? You think it's a fucking joke? Well it ain't funny pal. Now get the fuck out of here and don't come back. I see you round here again I'm going to break your sorry-ass legs!"

Men started gathering around the area, giving him sarcastic, pathetic looks.

"But Sheriff, I'm telling the truth. It was me. I did those murders, the one at the bar and the one at the little store, and last night I killed a gang of three in my apartment. I shot them all." At this, Markovic burst into laughter, as did the fat officer, and the others that had gathered around them.

"We've got the bar and store murderer. But if what you're saying is true, then I'm supposing that you know where the murder weapon is. Do you have it on you?" said the Sheriff, a sarcastic smirk on his face.

"No, actually, I…I'm not sure where it is."

"Why am I not surprised?" he said "And the bodies, of that gang of yours. Will we find them in your apartment?"

"Uh, no. I…I don't know, they've disappeared!" He said, with no conviction, knowing that he must have sounded absurd. "Look, I've killed them. Please take me in!" Guy was offering his wrists for the Sheriff.

"Boy, you're really testing my patience now. If you're looking for the loony bin you are a bit late, it moved! Now out!" he grabbed Guy's shirt and dragged him out of the station. He pushed him to the ground.

"Crazy son-of-a-bitch," he said, spitting at the floor.

Guy stood in front of the building, carved writing above the main entrance declared that the Police are "There to Protect, Serve and Honor the town's folk". Guy shook his head in dismay and sighed. This was hard to digest. He had not contemplated anything beyond giving himself up to the police. He had not expected that to go wrong. He was angrier than ever now, now that all he wanted was for this madness to end. But what had happened just then, in there, brought in new doubts, more insane questions. Did what happened last night really happen? If it did, what happened to the bodies, to the guns, to the blood? And why didn't he tell the Sheriff about killing Barton as well? It did not make any sense, none of it.

"I'm sick of this. This is insane. It can't be real," he whispered to himself, "I've got to end it." There was only one other option. But before going ahead with it he had to do one more thing. He would go back to his parents' home, one more time. Firstly because he'd promised his mother that he would, because he wanted to say his final goodbye; secondly because he wanted to confront his father, about his behavior towards him, about the photo.

There, just outside the station, parked alongside the pavement was a new-looking Ford hatchback with its engine running. Someone had left it there, its hazard lights flashing. Guy seized the opportunity and without thinking twice, having nothing to lose and no-one to stop him, ran to the car, climbed in and drove off, heading to Blossomville.

It was frightening, the sight of that damned, forsaken place. It looked exactly the same, just as she remembered it from that tragic morning.

As she was making her way out of the van she could feel her heart weakening, her mind slipping. She could still remember the horrible feelings she'd had. She could still hear the gunshots. She could still see Aaron, lying there on the filthy floor, his blood everywhere. Patrick held her hand as they walked towards the small, rugged building.

Upon closer inspection, Christina noticed that the windows of the store were very dirty, un-cleaned, left to gather dust. Rubbish spilled over from the couple of bins placed in the right corner of the store, along with several cartons and rubbish sacks. The two stopped at the door for a moment, not speaking a word. It was like each of them knew what they were here for without saying. Patrick squeezed Christina's hand and together they stepped in.

Just before turning back, Patrick saw what he believed was a twisted vision, one of his crazy hallucinations. He'd not had one for quite a while, but this time, it was a flash. It was more like the remembrance of a long forgotten dream that surfaces with a rush all of a sudden. He didn't panic. He didn't get scared. He simply embraced it and accepted it. He was calm. Because it made sense and because something deep within him said it was alright.

This is what he saw: He was in a vast, empty, hilly land. He stood there unmoving, sensing great danger. Beside him was a woman. He was holding her hand. Even though he did not look at her, he knew it was Christina. They stood there, anticipating something. And it came from the sky. A great star falling, burning in red flames, making the black starless night-sky glow. Then it crashed in the yonder, a big explosion rattling the earth and the sky, giving birth to a mushroom cloud that expanded and rose higher than the eye could follow. A moment later and he could see figures hovering above him, of different sizes and shapes. These black, soulless shapes were of men and women, dead and faceless. But there was someone else now, standing right in front of them. He was not there before. This man looked weird. He was short and fat and had some hair on the back and sides of his head and a moustache like Hitler's. He reminded him of something. He looked familiar. He had seen him before.

That man, as they walked into the store, was standing right there in front of them. He sat behind the cashiers till.

It was John Pinkerton.

Chapter 30

▼

To verify his latest discoveries, Officer Randy Challenge had to visit the Pinkertons one more time. He headed to Highway 11, to the couple's store, all on his own, not even saying a word to the Sheriff. If what he had come across was true, he wasn't sure he could risk trusting Markovic.

There was definitely something fishy going on, he was certain of that now. The way this whole shenanigan unfolded was a mystery, nothing seem to fall into place. It was only when he realized that there was no place to fall into in the first place that it started making sense. It must be a cover up for something greater. Or someone. Where the two killings fitted was another mystery. And the fact that he was denied access to the murder suspect they'd captured, the tramp with the previous "violent record", fed on his suspicions. The mean ole Sheriff was hiding something, holding back on information, keeping this case very close to his chest, which was very unlike him. Randy couldn't help but think that this was more than just a murder case for Markovic—not that he had come across many—this was personal.

The day before, late in the evening, when the station had been almost completely deserted, apart from the odd one or two officers, Randy had overheard a conversation coming from the sheriff's office. Markovic had been speaking to someone on the phone, he couldn't figure out whom, but he seemed important, big. Randy had overheard the Sheriff mentioning Mr. Pinkerton and something involving a handsome sum of money. He was ratty and very disgruntled, but he was sure he could "handle the situation". It was all too bizarre to the young officer. He had not much experience under his belt and he'd certainly not seen his share of the business, but he was still sure this wasn't the way to go about things, all behind locked doors and in whispers and secrecy.

The connection was there. Some pieces of the puzzle were actually coming in together quite well now; the money and Mr. Pinkerton, along with what he had learnt from Mrs. Pinkerton, and of course Lock-Up, the small security firm downtown, meant that there was something between the two. Pinkerton had to know something, something that the Sheriff wanted to keep hidden. Oh yes, there was some conspiracy going on. Randy had to admit it, he didn't expect such an eventful time when he was first assigned to be part of the small police force of the sleepy, zombie-like Okay, the forgotten county. He had never expected to come across something with earth shattering, life-changing potential.

As he approached the store, he was wondering if he was going to find the Pinkertons still there or if they had decided to make a run for it. But that was unlikely, bearing in mind Mrs. Pinkerton's condition, unless Mr. Pinkerton was planning on leaving her alone and disappearing. He tried to calm himself down and stop his wild, uncanny presumptions, he would find out the truth soon enough

The delivery van was parked just a few meters from the store. Randy approached slowly, stopping behind the van. He was suddenly anxious. There was something about that van, he wasn't sure what but had a hunch, his policing intuition kicking into gear. He ran a quick plate number check over the radio. The van wasn't registered. He made sure he didn't give away his location to the radio operator, just in case.

Randy got out of his car and walked towards the store, his hand on his holster.

It was like walking into your own grave. For a second you feel life slipping away from you and dissipating into the void, through a tunnel of heartache and black pain. Like the world melting into a little, colorful puddle, old and small and lonely; the puddle of your dead lover's blood. And the only way to survive it is by holding your breath, closing your eyes and wishing that you were drowning down to the deepest depths of the puddle to meet your lover at the bottom.

Christina kept squeezing Patrick's hand tightly, as she walked across the floor. She realized that she couldn't remember much of the place; she was in such a state that nothing registered in her mind. The inside of the store seemed like one of those places you find yourself in a quixotic dream, a place where you know you have been before but cannot familiarize yourself with, a place stripped of logic and time and space, as if the it was just the idea of the place that you are familiar with, not its actual existence. She looked around, adjusting her eyes to the gloomy, poorly lit interior. She came to the conclusion that the store had been neglected for quite a while. She then looked at Patrick. He was staring down at the floor; she followed his eyes down to the dried, dark stain that was once Aaron's blood.

"Yes, that's real blood. Friggin' thing can't be wiped off with nothing. Tried everything, I did." said John, standing behind the cashier desk, in his filthy shirt and overalls. "That'll be a dollar." He added.

"Excuse me?" said Patrick.

"To take a picture," he said, like a bored tourist guide.

Christina broke down then. She dropped to her knees, sobbing. She gently grazed her hand over the stain, not daring to touch it. A tear fell down her cheek onto it. Her wet tear moisturizing the dried blood. John suddenly recognized her the second he heard her cries. He rose from behind the desk and started making his way slowly to her.

"It's you," he said. "I'm sorry. I...I didn't know."

Patrick, doing his best to tend to the grieving young woman, gave the shopkeeper a mean, angry look. "Bastard," he muttered. John felt very ashamed and angry with himself, the sight of that beautiful woman crying her heart out almost broke his. He didn't say anything else. Patrick helped Christina get up on her feet again, wiping her tears, gathering herself. She'd promised herself she was going to be strong and she was planning on keeping that promise. She regained her composure, took a deep breath and stared at John.

"You know who killed Aaron," she told him. It was not a question. "I think I know who he is too, but I want to be certain." The look in her eyes sent shivers through his spine, never had he seen eyes so endearing, so full of determination and strength and passion. He couldn't refuse her eyes.

Just as he was about to speak the door opened. A figure emerged, blackened by the sunshine.

"Mr. Pinkerton?" the figure called.

"Oh shit!" John said, turning around to make a run for it. They had come for him. The bastard sent someone to kill me, he thought.

"Hey!" shouted Patrick at him.

"DON'T MOVE!" shouted the figure. As Patrick turned to face the door, his metallic watch caught the sun, glinting into the eyes of the person at the door.

"POLICE! FREEZE!" Officer Randy Challenge wasn't about to take any chances. He made a quick call, a snap decision. He had to. He was jittery, didn't know what to expect. He'd never been in real action. His mind was set. The glint, he decided in his rash judgment, was a weapon, probably a gun. He had to act fast. He pulled out his Gloak and fired straight at Patrick.

Christina screamed in horror. "It's happening again", she thought, and ducked to the ground, covering her head with both hands, while Pinkerton dived back behind the desk.

Patrick fell to the ground.

Guy was determined this time to confront his parents, his father in particular. He wanted him to answer all the questions he had about why he treated him so harshly, so indifferently, over all the years. And he wants to confess and come clean, tell them what *he* has done, everything. The gun, the killings, the stranger whose face he deformed for nothing more than stepping on an ant, the strange accident, the stolen car, which he was now driving toward home in and finding to be very comfortable.

"I suppose I could have taken the bus", he thought to himself, "but why settle for less when I can actually get away with murder". He shook his head and chuckled. The irony of it all. Life. And all its bullshit. He was so on the edge that he wouldn't be surprised at all if he had woken up in a female alien body on Venus to realize that all this was a stupid, silly dream. He was driving like mad now, taking the car's speed to the limit, reminiscing about the day he crashed, and dodging cars. He wanted to get there fast.

As he arrived in Blossomville he wondered if he should just keep going, keep driving and driving and driving through the deserts and mountains until he reached the end of the world, if he should leave his parents living their normal lives without having to know what sins their mad son had committed. They have Morris after all. He'd surely keep them happy. Driving into the district, through its abandoned, filthy streets, passing by the occasional yobs, some giving him dirty looks, others completely ignoring him and carrying on with what they're doing, Guy saw two teenagers in rugged clothes "playing" with a stray dog, with a stick, while a naked little boy ran away, crying, calling for his mommy.

He took the right turn into Rosegarden Street. He couldn't believe he was back again in such a short time. It felt very strange. There was a fancy, black car parked on the other side of the street, there seemed to be a person behind the wheel. He wondered whose car that could be, certainly no one from the area, unless someone had won the lottery jackpot. He would have thought that a car like that would have attracted a lot of attention.

Guy parked his stolen car alongside the pavement, in front of his old home and got out. He took another look at the flashy, German car. The sun was warming up now, as the day progressed.

He walked towards the house, through the gate and through the dead front garden. The house looked very sad. Guy felt like hugging it, a silly thought he knew. But that's what he would have done if only he could.

As he stood facing it though, he sensed danger. A bitter-cold wind blew from the west and the house began changing; the world around him was changing. Suddenly the clear blue sky was gone and there were black, menacing clouds coming up from behind the house, which was now transforming into a monster, growing arms and feet made of old trees and earth. It grew a mouth as deep and dark as a cave, with bulky sharp teeth of black stone. And it grew bigger and bigger, or perhaps he was shrinking to a tiny, little thing. Guy was frightened; the whole house was now a great monster, full of malice and evil. And it was about to eat him. Just as it was about to reach out its hands, creaking and crackling, to get him, there was a noise. It brought Guy back to reality. He looked back to see that the man in the flashy car was now out, standing with his hands folded across his puffed chest, wearing a black suit and dark sunglasses. He was bald.

When Guy looked again at the house, it was as it should be, his parents home, his old house, dull and lifeless and very much regular. He walked in, hoping to find his mother and father sitting together in the living room. They were.

She was sitting alone on the sofa, her hands clasped together on her lap. She had a weary look on her face. His father was sitting on his special chair, his back to Guy, with cigar smoke lingering above his head.

"Hello mother," he said.

"Hello dear."

"How are you doing dad?" he asked, walking slowly into the center of the room.

"Oh I'm fine son," said his father "I've missed you."

Guy frowned. Looked at his mother. She looked down, not meeting his eyes. This was strange; his father's voice was completely different. It didn't sound at all like his.

"Dad?"

Guy took two more steps closer to the chair and stood in front of it. His eyes widened, lungs hardened and felt his heart freezing over as he saw the man sitting on his father's chair.

Chapter 31

The man sat luxuriously on the ancient chair, his legs crossed, holding the cigar between index finger and thumb, toying with it. He puffed the smoke up towards the ceiling. His smart, posh suit had an extraordinary gleam, his receding gray hair seamlessly kempt back. He had a wicked, sickening smile on his face. A very famous smile it was.

Guy stood in front of him, not believing his own eyes. Of course he was expecting something, after what happened just before walking in, he had a feeling all along. But it struck him just as bad. It was growing clearer and clearer every second he stared at that face. He could feel his shirt soaking wet with sweat. His forehead seemed to be on fire. He had a rush of emotions surging through.

"It can't be!" he whispered.

The man sitting in his father's chair, smoking his father's Cuban cigar was the Mayor of Okay, Leon Cunningham.

"Mother? Where is Dad?" Guy asked, his eyes fixed on the Mayor. She didn't reply. Kept her head down. Guy turned to her sharply.

"Look at me mother," he told her with renewed venom "Where is my father?"

Carter Jay Kelton walked into the room through the kitchen door, wearing the same clothes Guy had seen him in the last time. He had his hands in his pockets, standing with defeated posture in the doorway. His face was sullen, as pale as the twilight horizon. He, too, looked down.

"Dad? What's going on Dad?" Jay remained silent, his eyes avoiding his son's. "*Dad*!" Guy shouted, "Say something. Tell me it's not true!"

Jay sighed deeply, swallowed hard and then looked straight at the boy he'd been made to accept as his son. Guy then trailed his gaze to his mother, her sad face animated with hurt and pain and shame. She looked back at her son, their eyes meeting for a fleeting moment, and then Guy's gaze drew to the Mayor, sitting there in his smart suit with his sickening smile.

Their eyes locked.

Nothing was said. Guy knew it. He struggled with it, fought it, and tried with all his might to deny it. But there was no escaping it. This confirmed his worst fears. This explained everything. This meant that his whole life was a lie, a fake; a meaningless, purposeless existence. It was true. He could see it in their eyes.

Leon Cunningham, The Mayor of Okay, was his real father.

Patrick lay on the filthy store floor staring up at the white, florescent-lit ceiling, wondering for a moment where the hell he was. He felt wetness in his left arm but couldn't move. All he could do was stare at the ceiling. He might have heard commotion around him, distant voices and blurry figures hovering over him. In that moment he believed he was swimming in a vast, endless ocean, beautiful and warm, with his mother and sister. They were happy, gaily laughing and giggling, calling for him to join them and not to drift afar. He was waving at them, calling out, trying to make them realize that he was actually trying to swim towards them, not away. But they couldn't hear him. And he drifted and drifted further and further until he couldn't see them anymore.

"Patrick! Please!" he heard a gentle voice say. He felt her hand supporting his head. He focused on her face and smiled in relief at the beautiful sight he saw, her captivating eyes, her luscious lips, and her perfectly shaped nose. Christina was still holding his hand, eyes still wet with tears.

"You're not leaving me too, are you?" she said with a brave smile. He shook his head, barely pulling a smile.

The figure that shot him, Officer Randy Challenge, was now sitting by his side, tending his wound. Randy could still feel the adrenaline pumping. He was a bit shaky. He had just shot a man for the first time. Luckily, it wasn't a fatal shot. The bullet simply grazed his left arm, leaving a large cut behind. It was actually the knock he got on the back of his head when he fell that proved more harmful than the shot.

"Ouch!" said Patrick, feeling the aftermath of the bump. Another bruise to show off.

"You're going to be fine," said the rookie officer, "It's just a cut. I thought you had a gun!"

"Oh that's ok," said Patrick, calmly, "been getting a lot of that lately."

"We're going to have to report this," said Randy, patching the wound with a piece of cloth and getting up, "I'm calling an ambulance,"

"No!" said Christina, grabbing his wrist.

"I have to, Ms. Heywood!"

"Please. Don't."

"But why?" he asked, "I almost killed an innocent man!" His spirits were dampened. He realized he's in big trouble now. He might be taken to court, taken off the force, even jailed. He knows that he blew it.

"We need your help," she told him. She looked at Patrick, now supporting himself on the desk. He nodded. "We came here to find the truth about Aaron Minister's death, my…" her voice faded then.

"We think we know who the murderer is," Patrick said "We also think that *he* knows," nodding towards John, who all this time was hiding behind his cashier desk.

The officer was puzzled. It couldn't have been a coincidence. What are these two really after? Who are they looking for? He was intrigued now. His spirit picked up and soon enough he forgot about the earlier incident and was again on the case, his mind calculating possibilities and probabilities.

"That was what I came here for in the first place," he said "To talk to him." He turned to face John and walked up to him.

John was about to wet his pants. He was frightened. He started talking, explained how he came across a very important revelation, about the recent murders. With that, he'd thought he could extort some money out of Markovic; $10,000 he'd alleged stolen by the murderer. He wanted to get away. He told them that he was planning to leave everything behind because he was sick of it, he was tired, he wanted to leave his wife and start a new life somewhere else, far from Okay. That's why he was very much convinced that Randy was here to kill him. The Sheriff had said he would "deal" with him if he didn't shut up, that no one would believe him anyway. Markovic, of course, was right, John knew. There was no way he could prove it. He regretted it all. He was stupid, a fool. His desperation was suddenly driving him to lengths he never expected he could even consider. He was now crying, sitting on the chair, his head in his hands.

"I hate him," he said "I hate him. He ruined my life. Ruined me. I wish he would die!"

"Who are you talking about?"

"That man, whoever he was. I don't know his name. I'm not even sure I know what he looks like anymore."

"Describe him, please," pleaded Christina.

"I don't know. He was very average. Black, short hair. Fit. I don't know. But I know that the police got the wrong man. They didn't even call my wife up to ID him. Not that she would have been much help; she's still very much traumatized. But I saw him driving away, in his car, the same car I saw in the papers the other day,"

Patrick knew it was him, but this was for Christina. She wanted to be certain.

"You know him? You said you did," asked Randy.

"Yes," replied Patrick, "I do. His name is Guy Kelton."

This wasn't enough, Randy wanted more proof, more answers. He wanted to carry out what he'd come here to do. He wanted to match what he had discovered with the other pieces of the case.

"Mr. Pinkerton," he began "Do you have a surveillance system operating in this store?"

The storekeeper was taken aback by the question. He thought for a second. "No. I mean, yes,"

"Do you?"

"Yes. But it's idle. Not operational," he said, pointing behind them towards the door, to the corner. There was a small CCTV camera installed there, difficult to spot between the shelves and cartons.

"It is, Mr. Pinkerton," said Randy, taking control of the situation, "The last time I was here, as you will recall, Mr. Pinkerton, I had interviewed your wife. Asked her a few questions. You were right, I didn't get much from her. But I found a paper tucked between the bed and the lamp-desk. That paper was from a security firm. They had repaired the system, setting a one-day trial. For her own reasons, your wife saw it fitting to not inform you of this. That one day, however, was crucial. It just so happened to be exactly the day of the murder."

Everyone was silent. They couldn't believe it. If that were true then they would have a videotape of the murderer, in fact the whole incident would have been caught on camera.

The video set was kept in one of the desk compartments. It was locked. They had to bash it in. It was there, and the videotape as well. There was a small television hung up to the right of the desk. Randy pressed the play button. Patrick, still feeling the sharp pain from the bullet, grabbed Christina's shoulder, shaking his head at her to not watch. She didn't move and kept her eyes on the screen. Her heart was racing, her teeth clenched.

The three men gathered around the small screen, their eyes unblinking, staring.

The time and date were in chubby white font at the top right corner of the screen. It'd started recording at 00:01am. The young Officer skipped through the early hours of the day to get to the time of the murder. A moment later a man appeared into view. It was Aaron Minister. Christina gasped, hand clasping her mouth. They could only see his back, but she would recognize him anywhere, anytime. The way he walked, what he wore. It was him.

A few seconds and he disappeared. Less than a minute passed before another man walked in, picks a few things very quickly and gets to the cashier desk manned by Mrs. Pinkerton. A few things were said. The system had no audio facility. The other man then walked out again, empty-handed, and after about twenty seconds he barged back into the store. He pulled out something and started waving it at the old lady, and then all of a sudden Aaron popped back into the screen. The other man now turned to him, facing the store door, facing the camera. There was no doubt about it now. It was him. In a flash he started shooting at Aaron.

Three silent shots.

Aaron dropped to the floor, knocking down one or two stands. Guy then ran off.

Tears were streaming down Christina's eyes, now turning red as blood. She broke down, trembling. Seeing the whole ordeal unfold in front of her own eyes proved substantially traumatic She had done everything she could to block that horrible memory from her head, yet now it played right in front of her eyes. Patrick was quickest to react after the initial shock. He wrapped his arms around Christina.

"Shut it off for Heaven's sake!" he urged.

Christina was now remembering the horrible dream she'd had, where she saw Guy take her lover away. She kept thinking about that day when she'd been only inches away from her lover's killer, outside the bookshop. It just dawned at her how close she came to that person. Guy Kelton. That was his name. She kept repeating it to herself. Why? What did he have against Aaron? Why couldn't he have just walked away? Why did it have to happen? Was it fate or simply another of life's injustices? She couldn't believe it. She had been about to leave it all and move on but one small incident had led to another, and now they were close to capturing the real murderer.

She looked up at Officer Challenge, challenging him with her eyes, with her words, full of sorrow, full of passion and anger.

"Get him."

"Get him!" he said, his voice echoing with vengeance.

He was now beyond angry; this has gone beyond mutual courtesy. He was about to put an end to it, to the years of political mayhem, and mischievous alliance they had formed. He couldn't allow this to go on. No more Mr. Understanding, there was no room for that anymore. God knows what could happen next, he thought to himself, as he sat behind his marble desk in his fancy modern office at the top of the Doyen Tower. His men, in their formal, black suits, stood in silence, paying full attention to their employer.

Spitfire had seen his share of enemies and ignorant rebels in the mobsters business, he'd taken them all out, and when he'd come to this town he'd come with a mind set on overtaking it. Nothing and no one was to slip through his fingers; not the small merchants, not the small-time crooks, not even the Mayor…and definitely not his pitiful son.

John Pinkerton was left to contemplate his own fate. Randy was now more determined to get to the bottom of this. When Christina jumped into his car he didn't even attempt to stop her. They exchanged glances. Nothing was said. Of course, Patrick wasn't about to let her go on her own. He wanted to see this through too, for his own reasons. They weren't far away now; Randy stepped on the pedal towards the forsaken suburbs. Patrick caught Randy's eyes on the rearview mirror. He read his mind.

"I know what you're thinking," he said "Guy Kelton. How do I know him? I don't know. I don't *know him* know him, if you know what I mean," he said. Both Christina and Randy waited for an explanation. "I first met him when I moved to live with my uncle in Blossomville. I say I met him, I mean I saw him. It's been such a long time. I've not stepped foot in that place ever since I left. I don't know. I don't understand it. It's not like we were best friends. He was just another kid in the block. We'd not even spoken once. We were complete strangers. I'd completely forgotten about him. His name, his face, they'd been lost, erased from my memory. But somehow, for some reason," he paused, not finding the words, struggling to make sense. "It's like there's a mystic connection between the two of us."

He stopped talking then and remained silent for the rest of the short drive, just looking out the window at the odd passing car and the odd bare tree. He tried to focus, concentrate on drawing these memories, trying to understand the relationship between him and Guy. There must be one, he was sure of that. But that's it. Perhaps, he wondered, the next meeting with him will provide more answers than questions.

As they got closer, Patrick began to give out directions he didn't expect he would remember so vividly. The place was not like he remembered it. It was such a shock, how a place can change so dramatically in such a short time. He was now very anxious as he felt the end approaching. It wasn't a pleasant feeling. He wanted to see the look on Christina's face. She did not speak a word; she was preparing herself for the final face-off. She suddenly felt vulnerable. She wanted go home, to find her mother busy in the kitchen making blueberry muffins.

"Turn there," said Patrick "It's the third from bottom."

Soon as Randy took the turn, all three of them realized there was something wrong. Getting closer, slowly, they were all on the edge of their seats. There was something black in the middle of the street.

When they were close enough, they could see that it was the body of a dead man.

Chapter 32

For the longest moment, that seemed to last like a long night's nightmare, they were all silent. The room was quiet as space. If you had dropped a needle then, it would have sounded like an erupting volcano. Jay Kelton still stood by the kitchen door, head down. His wife sat still on the sofa, trembling; also head down. Leon Cunningham still sat on the chair, the cigar burning between his fat lips. Guy was frozen, as if nailed to the floor, his eyes twitching. The atmosphere was deadly intense.

Guy's mind was burning, taking in this astonishing revelation, trying to grasp the gravity of its reality. He knew it was true, but he simply couldn't accept it.

"Is it true?" he asked again. "Tell me it isn't, father." The last word he said pleadingly, turning to Jay, looking all old and frail and helpless.

"Why do you think you're still here?" said Cunningham. "Why aren't you in jail? You know the police could have simply picked you up. There were plenty of witnesses. You've killed a lot of men. Notably Barton and GoGo and his men. That wasn't a smart move. You've pissed some bad people, son. That's why I'm here. I've protected you all this time, but I can't do much more. You have to leave Okay...for good."

Guy was still struggling. His head about to explode, anger brewing within. He felt as if the ground beneath his feet was giving way, as if it was evaporating under him, revealing a bottomless pit, rapidly dropping into it. It was all rushing too fast, cramming up his senses. His breathing became toilsome. Anxiety seeped through. It was true, Leon Cunningham, the Mayor of Okay, was his father. But the more burning question was *how*?

Only now, at that particular torrid moment, what he had seen behind the gray gate became clear. It had settled in the back of his head, but he'd not given it a second thought ever since. When he'd walked through that gate, he'd walked into a world of intolerable pain, a world where human suffering is manifested in the most grotesque manner. It was as if he were in hell, crossing a bridge over a sea of lava and fire, filled with burning souls. He was then in a black place, a very dark, wall-less room. There was a beast—that for some reason made him think of a cunning lion—so menacing and violent, viciously devouring a small rabbit—which for another reason made him think of his mother. The beast, he realized, was his father.

When he was in that place none of that had made sense, but now that he could put the pieces together, he understood.

Leon Cunningham had raped his mother, twenty-five years ago.

That would explain the awkward years of growing up, why his father treated him like he had, why his mother always had this sad, serene look on her face, why his father—or at least the man he always believed was his father—favored his older brother and treated him more properly as a son. It explained all the weird things in his life. It was devastating. His whole worthless existence became even more sour and doomed with this revelation. It hit him hard. He looked at his mother. She was crying, ever so gently, quietly. He felt his own tears welling. He felt anger taking over. Rage. Hatred.

"You bastard!" he said, leaping at the Mayor, grabbing him by the neck and pulling him off the chair. "You fucking bastard!"

"No!" his mother yelled out, pleading to him to let him go. Cunningham pushed him off and pulled himself free.

"Yes. Listen to your mother now son," he said, smartening himself up, his suit, his tie, his hair.

"I am going to kill you," declared Guy with clenched teeth, hands into fists, ready. Cunningham laughed, such a hoarse, ugly laugh.

"Oh yeah! Come on, kill me. Right here in front of your Mommy. Kill the Mayor. Kill your *father*." He said sarcastically. Then pointing at Jay he continued: "Look at that sorry, worthless piece of shit. He was nothing. He is nothing. He's always been nothing. And she still chose him. Him over me! After all those years of loyalty to him and love for her, they gang up on me. They want to destroy *me*. Oh no. I wasn't going to let that happen. Yes sir, I wasn't." He now moved to the window, looking out, checking on his guard outside, in the car. He turned around again, looking at Jay with hateful eyes.

"We were destined for greatness you and I, Jay. We had plans. We were going to run this place like Big Ben. But then you go and do what you did. You have any idea how that felt? I hope these last twenty-five years helped make you understand. Watching your wife raped, your career destroyed, your whole life taken away. I hope that every passing second of these years felt like a nail through your skin, every breath you took like acid-gas in your lungs, every time you looked at the mirror, you looked at her, you looked at him." He then turned to Guy, walking up to him, looking him in the eye.

"You can't kill me son. You are here because of me. Without me you are like them, nothing. Now you have to leave. Don't worry, it'll all be fine," he said, a smirk on his face. "Trust me."

Tears were now streaming like a river down Guy's cheeks. He'd given up, he was defeated, his spirit choked to death. It was as if he was limbless, helplessly numb.

"You ruined everyone's life. How could you? How could you live with yourself? Do you have any idea? Do you care?" Guy said, almost in a whisper, his voice weak and fragile. "You've hurt my mother." He looked at his mother, sobbing now, her face buried in her hands. Guy broke down; he fell to the floor, his head failing him, his heart aching, broken to tatters. Why? He thought to himself, why me? Should I have existed in the first place? Am I meant to be here? My mother. My poor, beautiful mother. He has been the misery in their lives.

"She deserved it," said Cunningham, prancing around the room, his head held up high. "So did that old, ungrateful man. You've heard of Mr. Jacker, son? He was going to betray my trust. The old fool. For all these years I paid him off to keep his gob shut and then suddenly he decides to have a conscience. People are stupid like that. You see, no-one threatens me, son. No-one dares. As your parents know full-well by now."

Guy now remembered something else, the dream he'd had of the alley and the gate and the old man. It must have been him, Jordan Jacker, the man found stabbed and electrocuted in a neglected filthy alley. He knew the secret, and he knew about the rape, he'd probably witnessed it. Over twenty years later he is murdered. Now it was clear why the case was forgotten, why no-one bothered about him.

Cunningham got closer to Guy, patted him gently on the head, and was about to leave, leaving a destroyed, broken family behind, when he heard someone calling.

"Leon!" Jay yelled.

The Mayor turned around to find his former friend charging at him like a mad rhino across the living room. It took no more than five seconds, not long enough for anyone to react. All that Guy and his mother could do was shout out "*NO*".

But that wasn't enough because by the time they had, Leon Cunningham was already dead on the floor, with a chefs knife stuck in the center of his chest.

The body lay still in the middle of Rosegarden Street. Officer Randy Challenge quickly pulled over and got out of the car.

"Stay there," he told Christina and Patrick. But both ignored his order and followed him. Randy ran up to the body. It was of a man with a big, muscular figure, his bald head shining under the sun, bruised and bleeding, a large deep cut across his face. Randy checked his pulse. He was alive! He lifted his head off the ground. The bodyguard groaned.

"Who did this?"

The guard was still struggling to maintain consciousness. The blow had been heavy and if it weren't for his massive body, it would have been fatal.

"It was Guy," he said, the words barely escaping him. "He took my gun. That way," pointing to the south. The officer was about to get up and go after him, but the guard pulled him back.

"The Mayor," he whispered, his eyes indicating the Keltons' residence. Randy, his instincts running amok, snapped at Patrick to call for immediate back up and ambulance assistance using the radio in the car.

"My badge number's on the dashboard!" he yelled out, darting towards the house. He pulled his gun, determined to keep his cool this time. At the doorstep he shouted out. "Police! Stay where you are. Do not move." He cautiously walked in, drawing his gun up. He found two people in the living room, both looked devastated, harmless, and very much powerless. The woman was sitting on a sofa, crying, and a man dropped to the ground, leaning against the wall. He seemed as if he were asleep, peaceful and distant. There was blood on his white shirt and his hands.

In the center of the room, lying on the cheap Persian rug was the dead body of the Mayor of Okay.

Randy stared at them. They weren't going anywhere. He felt very sorry for them. He wished he could help them, but they were beyond that now. He dashed out of the house, and ran like mad to the south.

Christina and Patrick followed him.

The Mayor's bodyguard had heard the scream coming from the house. He'd started running towards the house. Guy saw him approaching from the window. He'd looked at his father, Jay, and looked at his mother, and then looked at the dead Mayor. He was glad he was dead but wished it had been himself who'd killed him. The fact that the Mayor was his real father didn't change anything. He was nothing to him. Just another person. Just another dead person. But his mixed emotions were still running wild within him, driving him mad. He had to act quickly; he knew that if that man came in he would probably kill all three of them.

Neither of his parents had said anything; they'd sat silently, aghast and perplexed, gaping at the bloodied, stout body of Mayor Leon Cunningham. His mother was trembling, having intense palpitations, and weeping. His father looked like a man who many years ago lost his pride, and now his sanity. Guy stood to leave, remembering the photograph he had in the pocket of his shirt. He took it out; looked at it one more time then dropped it on the mayor's dead body.

"I love you mother," he'd said to Mary-Moon, then looking at Jay "I love you father."

He'd jerked the knife out of the mayor's chest and headed out. As he made for the door he noticed his father's old bat, hung up on the wall in the tiny entrance hall—he wondered how he didn't see it on his first visit. It was the same bat that he begged his father for, the bat that Jay would never let his son touch. He stared back at his mother.

"Mother?" he said, "*I* killed the mayor. You understand? It was *me*." And then he'd walked out the door, through the glum garden and straight towards the muscular figure in the black suit, now standing in the middle of the road.

"Hey!" he'd called to Guy, reaching for his weapon. But before he knew it, Guy was only a few inches away from him, a knife in hand. It happened in a flash. Guy swung hard at him, slashing him across the face, knocking him down. The cut ran from the top side of the guard's head down to his chin. Guy then picked the guard's gun and threw the knife into the garden.

Then, Guy had started running. He'd run and run and run. There was only one place he could go.

Patrick had difficulty keeping up. His wound was still pretty fresh and it stung like hell. He grabbed it tight and with every step he took it stung even worse. Christina was now right behind Officer Challenge. He had no idea what was going to happen next. He'd just found the Mayor dead, murdered in one of Blossomville's slums. What on earth was going on? He thought. He didn't have good knowledge of the area and soon enough he found himself lost, no sign of Guy anywhere. He looked both sides. Nothing.

From some distance behind him, now almost catching up, Patrick yelled: "Straight ahead! The baseball pitch!" and off Randy went, not doubting his assumption. Sure enough, when Randy got to the pitch, Guy was there. How Patrick knew that, nobody knew.

Guy stood on top of the mound, looking up to the sky. It was lovely. The pretty white clouds sailed across the blue sky, sheet upon sheet, wave after wave, and fluff into fluff, the golden bright sun was shining onto the dried, scruffy grass, bringing life to it, its rays ever so softly warm. Guy had never seen a day as beautiful as this in Okay.

He wished he could smile.

Suddenly, he was a little boy again, doing what he did best, playing ball. He was throwing unstoppable pitches, strike-out after strike-out. He was hitting home-runs by the dozen. He was holding the ball in his fist, feeling its smooth surface, its padded lines. His father was watching him, watching him play, from behind the big chestnut tree.

Strangely, he could feel no more regrets. His soul was peaceful. Right there and then he felt he was complete, that he had fulfilled what he was here for, that now his time was up. He had to leave.

Randy drew closer, aiming the gun at him. The officer did his best to keep Christina and Patrick at bay, telling them to back off. He very slowly started taking small steps towards Guy.

"Drop your weapon Mr. Kelton, please," he urged, "There's been enough killing. Lets just stop it right here." He was discovering a new confidence in himself now. He realized that if he did not take the initiative and take control of the situation, not just in this case but in this whole pathetic, fallen town, no one else would.

"Drop it now!"

Christina came right behind Randy, looking at this Guy, this cold-blooded murderer with awe. Patrick stayed behind, despite wanting badly to speak with Guy again, having a horrible feeling of knowing exactly what was coming.

"Miss Heywood, *please*, get back there," urged Randy, sternly, his eyes still focused on Guy. Again, Christina ignored his orders. She stared at him. Locking her eyes onto his. "This is the man who took my lover away, took away my life. I should want him dead", she told herself. But strangely enough that wasn't how she felt. She saw things in his eyes, things that softened and hardened her heart at the same time, she saw pain and suffering and frustration and confusion, but she also saw fragility and love and despair. She hated herself for thinking about it even for the smallest moment, but all she honestly wanted then was to hold him.

Patrick felt the connection clearly now. He realized that he shared something with Guy, something deep and dangerous. Something that he might one day just comprehend the purpose of. One day, but not today.

Guy found himself wondering what it was all about. So many unsolved mysteries, so many impossible conundrums. As hard as he tried to make sense of it, and as bad as he wanted to, he simply couldn't come up with anything. He didn't care anymore. He wanted it to stop. He wanted all these dreams and visions and thoughts and atrocities to end.

He was in a quixotic daze.

Guy looked up again. He raised his arm up to his head. One more to go, he thought to himself. One more thing to do on this stupid planet. He pressed the muzzle against the side of his forehead. He thought he heard people shouting, yelling something at him. Never mind.

He thought of Jay, his father. He thought of his wonderful mother. He thought of his estranged brother. He thought of the men he killed, the silly bartender, and the nice young man at the store, the disgusting drug dealer, and the thugs in his apartment. He thought of Mr. Pickles, of Mrs. Jacker, of Lucia, the waitress, and he thought of so many things.

But the last thing that came to his mind, before the eternal darkness, was Angela.

Chapter 33

▼

He died instantly. There was nothing anyone could do about it. The three stood there in shock—feeling some sort of relief, for this ordeal had finally come to an end—looking at his dead body splayed on top of the baseball pitch mound, blood spilling onto the filthy white plate.

Randy wasn't angry for not being able to stop him from taking his own life. Christina didn't shed a tear. Patrick knew more or less it was going to happen.

He walked up to Christina and wrapped his healthy arm around her shoulders. Together they walked away from the pitch. Randy didn't try to stop them. He walked up to the body of Guy Kelton and secured the gun. Then he waited for the back up.

It was yet another bloody day in Okay.

The news came as a shock to the clueless citizens of Okay. It disrupted their fake peace and tranquility and delivered an electrifying wake-up call, making them suddenly more aware and conscious of the going-ons in their town. The impact was horrific and it jolted everyone from his or her zombie-like existence. There was a new air, a fresh and new era, it was like Okay County was reborn, handed a lifeline, a new beginning. People became less indifferent, more aware of each other's actions and their effects. It was a revolution—a bloody one at that—that rose for all the wrong reasons.

It is amazing how, when faced with horrific realities, people become united. Perhaps that had been Guy's purpose in existence. Perhaps after all it was his destiny, unwillingly and sub-consciously, his hatred, despair and disgust at life, was, ironically, the driving force behind the recreation of a better one.

Sometimes blood must be spilt for life to prosper.
And sometimes things do not have to make any sense to be true.
Sometimes life is without meaning or purpose or reason.
Sometimes life is dreams, sometimes it is chaos, others it is just that; life.

The blood on Carter Jay Kelton's shirt and hands wasn't proof enough that he had murdered the Mayor. The murder weapon, a sharp, chef's knife, was found in the garden with Guy's fingerprints all over it. Jay didn't confess and Mary kept quiet and was vague in giving details about what had happened, the truth of it being that she honestly didn't remember much of it. The Mayor's murder was, along with the other murders that had occurred, accredited to the couple's son, Guy Kelton.

Jay and his wife moved away to live with their son, Morris, and his new wife, on the other side of the country, leaving the madness behind and dumping the awful past in Okay. They made a full recovery from the traumatic incidents and are now leading a quiet, pleasant life.

Patrick Roymint and Christina Heywood also moved away. They were never seen again after that day. They are believed to be somewhere in Eastern Europe, he writing a book, she teaching English to children. Christina was contacted by her long-lost father after news of her mother's death reached him. He'd been living the past twenty years or so in the West Coast. She spoke to him but didn't meet him. She promised that one day she would. Patrick stopped seeing things.

Mandy Gray was killed in a mysterious car accident on the outskirts of the county just two days following the events of *that* day. Rumors circulated about her involvement in a huge drug scandal with the late Barton.

Officer Randy Challenge somehow managed to stage a complete coupe, with the help of some powerful friends from Internal Affairs. Sheriff Markovic was taken off the force without pension and has since disappeared. Randy was the strongest candidate to make the rare jump straight into Sheriff-hood, for his role in bringing this case to a satisfying and just conclusion.

John Doe, the tramp who was unlawfully charged with the murder of two men, was released and cleared of all charges. He is now back living in his filthy shed in Kingland.

Spitfire's men didn't get there in time on the day and the two men they were after were already dead. The result was very pleasing and satisfactory for him, it worked out for the best. Suddenly, the prospect of being Mayor of Okay wasn't a bad idea and not a far-fetched one either.

Leon Cunningham was portrayed as a wonderful, loving, caring Mayor who was needlessly and ruthlessly murdered, during a duty call to the abandoned suburbs of Blossomville, by a hateful and ungrateful crazy young thug with violent tendencies and mental disorder.

Mr. and Mrs. Pinkerton, now fully recovered, are still running their 'Jo & Jo' store on Highway 11.

Pickles is to this day looking after the same apartment building, in which Mrs. Jacker is still residing with her three children.

Angela continued to practice her harmonica to become a better street performer, under the supervision of her demanding father, on the pavements of the Morning Market.

Every morning she wonders if she will ever see that funny man with the funny name again, and if she will ever hear another of his lovely tunes.

Coming soon...by the same author:

Wonderful Things (A collection)

0-595-32761-3

CPSIA information can be obtained
at www.ICGtesting.com
Printed in the USA
BVOW08s1719031216
469602BV00033B/79/P